Time Of The Wolf

Alice E Wright

Alice E Wright

Contents

Chapter 1
Coffee Interruptus

Damn, damn, damn there's one here. I can smell it. Heaving a heavy sigh I look around and assess my surroundings. The coffee shop is jammed full of customers this morning. At least a dozen. Plus the four staff working behind the counter. Things could get ugly real quick if this thing goes full zombie in here.

My mate and partner is out in the car. Picking up my cell phone I text Ellan, telling her the situation. She responds right away with "So what's our play?

"It's your call." I reply "Let's just get our coffee, pull back and watch. There's too many in here to sort safely."

"Fine with me Liam, but I really wanted to go to the warehouse store today damn it".

"We may still have time." Even as I reply to the text, I can feel her rolling her eyes at my response.

By the time it's my turn to order I have located and identified which customer is the Myrna. He's waiting for his order, scrolling through his cell phone's feed just as calm and placid as any other customer. But my nose knows who it is. Myrna's give off the unmistakable odor of just ripe aged meat and that's just before really turning into ravening crazed killing zombies.

I text my wife again with the fellow's description and we fall into our comfortable familiar pattern of following the soon-to-turn zombie Myrna.

Getting our coffees, I exit the shop, following the still walking body while he slowly performs the task his body last remembers. Somehow managing to get into his own van and drive off, we follow behind. We don't have to worry about keeping back or giving him any distance, he isn't looking for people following him. His brain or muscle memory or whatever is driving him to function is only thinking about achieving one task. Thankfully for those around, in life, this guy appears to have been a safe driver.

I am hurriedly undressing in the back of our van, making sure to remove all of my clothing. Especially my leather belt. Those really suck when you are shifting forms if you don't get them off in time.

It takes me around fifteen minutes these days to fully shift to my wolf form and sadly it'll be a couple of hours before I am able to shift back after we've completed the kill. This getting old sucks. My wolf form is grizzled and gray and the 250 pounds of me is on the larger end of the spectrum. My browns and grays however, are well suited to the landscape in our Arizona desert. Even the slash of white across my face tends to blend in well with both the light and shadows.

"Are you ready honey?" My wife asks over her shoulder from the driver's seat. I give her ear a quick whiffling nuzzle in response.

We've followed the Myrna for what seems like a really long time down the freeway and through the city streets. Most of these things, once hitting the Myrna state of dead, can't hold a pattern that long. I'm not sure what that says about this one.

Finally he pulls into a mostly empty parking lot. The building looks like it is closed for the weekend. All the glass gleams and metal shines. The several stories show logo's of different businesses indicating it's some kind of office building. Deliberately getting out of the car our target walks slowly to the double glass doors, phone in one hand, coffee in the other. He stands there for what must be a full two minutes scrolling thru his phone while sipping his cup of coffee, pulling now and again on an obviously locked set of doors.

Suddenly he drops both his coffee and his cell phone. There seems to be an audible pause while we watch the scene unfold. His placid stare at the stubbornly locked doors ends when he grabs both handles and begins shaking them violently, yanking on them and screaming like the proverbial banshee.

"That's our cue." Ellan says, exiting our vehicle. I follow behind her coming thru the break between the front seats and out the door she has left open for me.

We split up. Ellan walks slowly and carefully towards the now maddened Myrna in his full zombie state. I stay off to his side out of his view. As is our usual teamwork Ellan starts whistling and clapping while raising her arms to attract his attention. He turns to look at the source of the noise and distraction. His pupils no longer react to light, his clothes look slept in now that I can see him more clearly.

Taking the bait he charges across the parking lot at her intentional disturbance. His single minded focus is on my wife, and he is completely oblivious to my intentionally slow and silent steps. He's made it halfway across the parking lot to Ellan who is still making noises and waving her arms to draw his attention but she starts backing up so I can begin my short but hopefully lethal dash. Getting in close enough to his side I launch myself at the moving target clamping my jaws tightly in a full-mouth bite on this newly turned Myrna zombies neck. My teeth meet as I crush flesh and bone with my bite, turning it into a mangled mess.

He never saw me and together we collapse into a heap on the rapidly warming Arizona asphalt. Sometimes it can take a few minutes for the brain to cease functioning and during that time it is very dangerous for us werewolves. We are crushing the entire neck and severing the zombies head from its spinal column to prevent nerves from sending messages down to the body. This in turn prevents these things from getting up and killing everyone in their path. Our hold on their necks instantly stops them dragging them down to the ground with us while these things are trying to return the favor by ripping the werewolf into many ribboned pieces.

Feeling my teeth close together I give a hard shake to be sure the spinal column is well and truly severed. Ellan walks up to us, looking me over carefully. She's looking for bites on me and to make sure this thing is no longer moving.

Smirking, my wife says "I think you got him." Releasing my hold, I step back. My muzzle as well as most of my neck are now lightly covered in the stinking black gore that a Myrna's blood congeals into.

"You know, it's at times like this I wish we could high five." I raise my paw waiving it in the air, she laughs. "Hey let's call this in and get you cleaned up." I agree. I haven't closed my jaws or licked my lips and I keep my head down so none of the foul gore that was once blood and plasma rolls down my throat. We walk back to the van and Ellan lifts the rear hatch, taking an ice chest filled with clean water out. Placing it on the ground for me, I wash my head and neck in it by dunking myself up to my ears and swishing my head around.

A security vehicle drives up for the companies or the building, I'm not sure which at this point. Looking at the body then he glances at me cleaning off the mess in the cooler. He makes a few notations on an electronic memo stick and drives off. Definitely a rent a cop as most off duty police officers stop and chat for a while.

Soon the lime green emergency services vehicle pulls into the parking lot. Randy, one of the states more well known and liked technicians steps out of the agencies repurposed ambulance's. Most local governmental agencies these days use them. Its more economical to keep them in service than to buy new. Randy's friendly easy demeanor makes him appreciated and well liked among both the werewolf teams as well as the survivors families whom he is partially responsible for notifying of their former loved ones final demise.

"Hey Ellan, you didn't call for a cleanup crew so they just sent me."

"We're good Randy, thanks. It went down clean today." Handing over her government issued identicard. Randy scans and tags this specific kill and subsequent payment to our account. He returns the card to her while I come around from the back of the van still dripping wet but now only from water and not the stinky black goo.

"Hey old man." Randy greets me. I lift my lip exposing a single eye tooth in a mock snarl falling into our comfortable routine. Smiling he pulls on his nitrile gloves from the depths of a pocket and turns to begin the normally grim task of positive identification of the remains including confirmation of Myrna status. Picking up the dead mans hand he runs the specialized memo stick over the back of the hand and down fingers confirming both fingerprints as well as vascular mapping for a positive ID. We only get paid when those get confirmed and then synced up with our scanned ID. This was a clean, textbook kill. Easy money. But even with that, it is never without some inherent risk to both partners, hence why it is mandated by the local alpha that wolves only work in teams of two but no more than three. Not that we generally allow mandates to be dictated to us. But it's a smart idea, and as such has merit we adhere to.

"We all good? Can we go now?"

Looking over at us he replies "Sure, he's all set and tagged. But do me a solid. I am obviously by myself, can you help me load this up?" Ellan turns and opens the side door of the van allowing me hop in to escape the rising temperature. Turning around I lay down to watch my wife and Randy work. It's good to get out of the rapidly warming Arizona day, the heat is hard on me and on werewolves in general.

"Of course."she responds. Being on the other side of fifty has never stopped her from the heavy work and as she walks over tells him "Happy to help, but you get the gooey end!"They smile comfortably and together get the two hundred pound corpse picked up and moved into the containment box still in the back of the vehicle. "You know that damn thing has wheels. We could have just brought it to the body." Ellan says. Not really upset, just a bit out of breath from moving a dead (pun intended) weight almost seventy feet. "Yeah well where's the fun in that?"

"Uh-huh" She huffs in mock displeasure. Randy busies himself with the requirements of his job while Ellan returns to the van closing the back hatch after dumping the cooler and returning it to its place to be cleaned and refilled at home. She returns to the drivers seat making sure the back air conditioner is blowing strong. She always looks after me. Looking at me in the rear view mirror she grins "At least I get to finish my coffee, this stuff is expensive! *Ha Ha!*" Putting the vehicle in gear and settling her sunglasses on, she drives us home, knowing I will need about another hour or so before I can successfully shift back to human.

Once home, I lay on the comforter thrown carelessly across the bed. I am an old wolf, fairly newly turned in the scheme of things. My grizzled muzzle, now clean of the mornings gore, rests on my paws while I follow my mate with all my wolfs senses. I worry for her. I mean when I pass on. Though not an alpha or even a second I am still far enough in the middle of any packs status to ensure some young pup will be quick to try taking advantage of my encroaching infirmities. But then my mate will be sure to dissuade any advantage seekers, at least for a while. This brings a smile to my eyes. She is as dominant as they come. More so than even the local alpha and this has made our lives together never without conflict or easy but I love her just the same....

I enjoy watching her in the shower. The water cascading down her while she washes the jobs dirt, grime and gore away. In her human guise she is tall with long brown hair and green eyes. A few more wrinkles these days, not as taught and firm and maybe if I am honest, her hair is more gray than brown really....but she's mine as I am hers.

Wolves don't live forever. Far from it. The same disease's that afflict humans afflict the wolves. Heart disease, arthritis, cancers, all of it. More slowly it was true and sometimes didn't that suck more. But none the less we are ravaged by time as every other creature on this earth eventually is. My wife is younger than me by a decade or so but has had some hard fights in her time, given her scars and not quite healed wounds that I know still pain her.

She finishes her shower in due time and begins towel drying herself. I have closed my eyes now to just enjoy listening to the normal sounds from within the house. The soft cotton of the towel rubbing against her body. The bathroom fan running softly in a vain attempt to keep the moisture at bay. Birds outside the over sized French doors flittering and chirping eagerly at the full feeders and of course the various hum of electronics from within the house itself.

·······

I keep a close eye on my mate and husband. I worry for him. Liam is getting older, slower and less responsive to threats. Even when I changed him, I knew it wasn't a cure. That time was not on his side. His heart was bad and he was out of other options. And it was not technically a sanctioned turning by the local pack alpha. But I love him and wasn't ready for him to leave me yet. And let's face it, I really don't give a tinker's damn about the sanctioning or not from the alpha.

I feel I need to protect him during the hunts now, but of course he wouldn't see it that way. He probably feels I am being overly cautious. But I once witnessed a couple of wolves who had been bitten during the early Myrna zombie hunts, and it was not good. Took almost an entire pack and a sharp shooter to ultimately bring the bitten werewolves down. But not before a lot of damage had been done. Innocents had been killed, pack members had been maimed and of course in today's world it had all been filmed for the newest social media craze to bandy their ever shrill cry to call all wolves a danger to society.

Demand for a national identification system along with public websites, like those for sex offenders was always a favorite topic in the news. It hadn't been easy to calm the craze from the last one. I love my mate too much to permit such a thing to happen to him, or our family.

Fully dried and dressed now I pick up my keys and with a smirk say "I'm still going to the store."

Chapter 2
Things That Go Bump

The younger ones were all faster, more agile, and Liam was old and getting older. There was something about the newer anti-serums, when given for the fifth and sixth times, that turned the living into zombies sooner and with less loss of faculties than before. They were still mindless. Relying on reflexes and muscle memory and basic instinct.

They could go through the motions most remembered or most often performed by their muscles. There's a truth to that muscle memory equation. More than most people give it credit for. It's how most people can type from only hearing the words without looking at the keys. It's why you can still ride a bike decades later as an adult or roller skate. And it is also why spirits or ghosts repeat. It is that unconscious, strongest memory. The mind-numbing repetitions that allow spirits to keep going even for centuries after their death. Their minds just won't let go. And it is why the Myrna zombies still do what they do. Early on, Myrna's were like the repeating ghosts of stories. Basically harmless, more a novelty to the general public. Eventually, they would fade away to nothingness and disappear. But the Myrna's were different. They were once human like a ghost but it's their body that's still hanging around instead of their soul. It has something to do with the way the mRNA antiserum reacted in the body after the fourth or fifth set of injections.

Since the governmental mandates in the early 2020s things had gone from bad to worse. It began as a rumor at first. The oldest in the population would be declared deceased except their eyes still followed the coroner's and their former caretakers. Eventually, too many grandmas and grandpas were caught on film "watching" after being declared dead, even from within their coffins.

At first, it was an oddity. Social media was alight with videos. Going to grandma's funeral while her eyes followed you. Great for content makers. But soon it became a public panic. Once the rumors were proven true and these so-called lifeless bodies that still moved became so common place that even the state run media's couldn't explain it away, it became almost comical. Almost.

But then things changed once again. Just a short decade or so later. The bodies got up. Tried to make coffee, get dressed, even go to work. And no longer was it the aged folks in their 70s or 80s, now it was folks in their 50s and 60s who still lived at home. They went to work daily, went to the gym, went shopping. All dead but still performing those functions their minds thought they should. Grieving families of the dead were eventually told to be quiet that this was just some sort of evolutionary jump. Yeah, right, some jump.

Over a few short years things got worse, got more complicated; messier. The Myrna's, nicknamed by a couple of popular social media sites, had become so common place most folks didn't even object when the governmental mandates called for a mass round-up order for them. Too many cameras, cell phones and video security showed how bad it was when these things eventually had their repeating patterns interrupted.

Remember that scene from the 1980's original ghost hunters movie where the librarian ghost got mad at the guys for interrupting her? Remember when she turned into this monstrous form? Myrna's are basically that ghost, only they become a zombie and attempt to kill you because well... they can. Once interrupted sufficiently from whatever their individual repeating pattern they were in, they basically go full zombie on you. There is some kind of explosive rage, a literal seeing of red and they bite, they claw, they rip, they tear flesh and they kill you. Then move on to the next living creature, whatever or whomever that is. They don't even have the decency to eat you like all the classic zombie movies say they should. And there is no ability to ever recover from their so-called interrupted state. They have to be "put down". That's where the werewolves come into the world.

Oh no, we've always been here. Remember all fables are bits of truth woven into stories. It's hard to discount literal centuries of stories from as far back as the Roman writer Petronius in 61 AD. He wrote in his Satyricon what may well be the oldest and first werewolf story.

We have hidden in shadows, in stories throughout time. I mean seriously, who wants to think that there are actually people out there who can change their form into that of an animal with six inch claws and fangs? And how exactly does that fit into their reality and religion? It scares humanity at a basic level. But nonetheless here we are. And when the Myrna's became so commonplace that human society could no longer deal with it we wolves stepped out of the shadows and into the light. Not really by choice. Again those damn cameras. Captured in all its gory glory was the first documented werewolf who stopped a rampaging Myrna in a coffeehouse line. Why is it always coffee houses? Apparently, they were out of her brew.

Sadly, not until the newly dead numbered a few more thanks to having their flesh literally ripped from their bones and their intestines exposed to sunlight for the first and last time of their early ended lives, was she able to be stopped. Turns out David, the werewolf who stopped the bloodbath, had been following this particular Myrna once he caught a whiff of her. It's the smell you know. The not quite decaying flesh and the stagnating gastric juices that no longer get churned and turned. It's a distinctly noxious odor we wolves can pick up pretty easily. It sets the hair along our bodies to vibrating, bringing out an involuntary snarl even in our human guise. But people bits and what looks like a bad horror movies gallons of blood still had the power to scare the average person. And so David became the first werewolf officially out. And oddly enough, he was not only welcomed, but hailed a hero that day. And the rest as they say, is history.

Chapter 3
All Good Grandma's Must End

The very next night a text comes through at a little after nine pm to my phone.

It reads - *Myrna rampage in home Scottsdale   Reply back to accept..*

Why does it have to be so far from our side of town? And wasn't there a closer team for crying out loud? I hear Liams soft even breathing coming from the far back bedroom, and decide to head out by myself. Without disturbing my sleeping partner I quietly retrieve my equipment in the form of a gun and sensible shoes. The gun is an older piece, my grandfathers' Ruger Security-Six. Heavy by most standards, but it's what I learned to shoot with all those years ago, and what I am most comfortable with. If I have to resort to using my weapon, the goal is a one shot stop. Smaller calibers tend to require multiple shots which means more chances to miss or just not take them down and I have zero intention of ever being bitten by one of those things. Heading out the door, grabbing my keys off the entry table I am careful to close the door softly so as not to disturb Liam.

Getting in the van, I plug in the address I have been given to my navigation. It's about a 55 minute drive. Would have been plenty of time for Liam to change I think. What on earth am I doing going out alone? This is how stupid things happen. Accidents which really aren't accidents, just poor choices. Yup that's me. Good choice central. Not.

I can remember back to being in the LA area when the local pack experienced a wolf who, having been bitten by one of these things, became a raging roaring ravening beast. A first as far as I was aware of and it was not good. As in capital NOT.

It took virtually the entire pack and finally a sharp shooter to bring the bitten wolf down. A few other wolves had been seriously and permanently mangled by the rampaging bitten wolf and other innocents had been killed. Somehow the bite of the zombie Myrna caused the werewolf to become a Myrna but not really. Still alive and with really big fangs and full control of his faculties. But that's not my plan.

Actually my plan is to just shoot the thing. Pretty simple I thought. More paperwork. I'd have to call the local cops and that's always a fun time. If the kill is a werewolf kill, I only have to call The Crows Nest for a clean up and body removal. They are the agency designated specifically to work with us. They do all the ID'ing right there, no paperwork. And payment is next day. But shooting them, while legally is an option, requires the involvement of the local law enforcement folks. And since it becomes an inter-agency cooperative thing, it cuts our bounty in half too. The nice thing is since we aren't pack, we don't share our fees with the local Phoenix packs general fund. Nor do I have to work under the Alpha's decree of two person teams. Well, technically speaking.

Getting there is quite the drive, first traveling east on the I-10 then the I-17 North to the Carefree Highway. My onboard navigation says its still about another 25 minutes travel time. Frowning I think "great, ten pm before I get there. I sure hope this is pop and done."

Eventually my travel leads me to unpaved dirt roads and multi-million dollar homes. I follow the navigation through a broadly arching open gate to the curved but graded dirt drive. Even though this is a one story home its towering front walls are filled top to bottom with glass all the way around, presumably for the view I am guessing. *"I'd hate to have their electric bill"* I think.

Usually night in the Phoenix area really isn't all that dark with the myriad of street lights, cars and businesses. But out here it is much much darker and quieter, which means I can hear the family inside. The Myrna, whom I can also hear, is actively tearing something apart and grunting while the family is apparently in another part of the home. I am best guessing since the windows and doors are still closed up tight and secure. Surprising how much sound today's good energy efficient windows can conceal.

I start forward, gun securely holstered to my side but within easy and quick reach. I freeze when a baby's wail reaches my wolf sensitive ears even through the still closed glass. The ensuing screech from the Myrna inside tells me he or she is done tearing up whatever victim it was working on and insures this isn't going to be as easy as I hoped. Up the decorative stone steps, I find the front door locked.

Sure, why not make it easy for the good guys, rolling my eyes, but I have to get in somehow without drawing this things attention and quickly. Following the flow of the homes stone steps to the back, I discover what had the Myrna's attention when I find the pieces of what is presumably the family dogs. Fur and blood and gore are all that remain. If I hadn't scented two dogs I couldn't have even distinguished that from the slimy mess that is now painted all over the back patio like some demented toddlers art. But I am grateful, if that's the right phrase, for finding the back sliding door standing wide open. Stepping around the mess, I enter cautiously but my enhanced senses tell me the whole group including the now terrorized family of four people plus the shrieking baby and one smelly dead rampaging grandma Myrna are all at the north side of the home. Why is she still in the home? Surely they realized she was dead. Maybe they are one of those families that thinks this is all some kind of sickness that will resolve. I can feel my eyes rolling again at the thought. It's a bad habit I have.

I follow the sounds and odor down the beautiful slate tile hall and find grandma Myrna actively engaged in attempting to break down the over sized bedroom door. Must be real wood or this thing would have shattered it by now. There are gouges in the wood, colored reddish black from both the animals blood as well as the Myrna's own fingers being rapidly de-fleshed from trying to scrabble through the door.

carefully and slowly removing my gun from the holster, I aim and could easily end this here and now, but am too concerned for the families safety to shoot. My sensitive ears tell me someone is bracing that door with their body.

My bullets are 158 grain jacketed hollow points and I know I can't miss this thing, in this hallway, this close. I also know the family is just on the other side of that door and I could easily hit one or more of them. Either I get this thing to chase me to another part of the house, a safer part to take my shot or I step back and change. Simple odds say this thing is faster and stronger than me in my human guise. While I am older, well past fifty with knees that complain most days grandma no longer feels pain in her joints. Adding I also have no idea about the layout of this house. I quietly step back, not drawing dead grandma's attention and open and exit the front door. I secure my weapon and hurriedly strip down so I can change. I push hard for a fast shift taking less than two minutes which hurts worse but I know I must hurry before circumstances can change again.

I am almost ready to re-enter the home. Waiting for the last of the kinks of the change to finish up, to permit me to move my limbs freely once again, to complete recreating me in its new form when for some damn reason an alarm starts blaring. Like really blaring, easily over 100 decibels. So much so within just a few seconds it becomes painful to my newly adjusted ears and as I cross the threshold, reentering the home on four paws things go wrong. Something must have popped in my ears because I can no longer hear well. Its' like hearing things from underneath the water, everything's muffled. But lucky me, the alarm seems to only enrage the grandma Myrna on to new heights which now include it turning to find the source of the new overwhelming sound. I'm now the closest in that assessment having taken what I had hoped to be a distraction, as an opportunity to sneak up on this thing.

In my head my new mantra is *not good not good not good*, as I turn to exit the building out the back, post haste with the rapidly chasing, re-energized and pissed off zombie in pursuit. I sprint across the side of the home and into the back yard again remembering there was a beautiful and huge pool back there. Do these things drown? I sure hope so.

Easily leaping across the six foot width of the pool to the other side, I turn in time to watch the Myrna run right into the waters and sink like a lead weight. I can't really stop to celebrate because much to my dismay, this is a newer pool with only a depth of about four feet. Staring in shock, I watch as grandma basically walks or slogs across the shallow depths as if in slow motion. Her gore covered clothing and arms now releasing its doggie bits and blood to float like a ring of death around her.

Easily crossing the space she begins making attempts to climb out while the water turns a lovely shade of, whatever blood bits, dog gore, wood shreds and black zombie goo is. Watching this thing try to climb out, I berate myself mentally *"Well hell, zombies don't breath do they. Guess that was an epic fail on my part, now what genius?"*

As if through a tunnel, I hear another car tear into the drive sending a small cloud of brown dust into the air and my attention is momentarily drawn to it. I recognize the sound of Liam's car. He comes sprinting around the side of the house, no easy feat for a man his age; surely being drawn by the splashing as I still can't hear too well. He stops short on the far side of the pool taking in the situation. Pulling his pistol he fires two rounds into the head of the semi swimming, mostly climbing Myrna grandma. She stops thrashing and just bobs there as nothing more than added debris now. The family comes stumbling out of the house through the still open slider, wide eyed and stunned.

Liam glances over at them shouting "Will someone please turn that damned alarm off?"

I drop down where I am at, hoping the alarm is turned off soon and await the local law enforcement as I am sure they have been alerted by now. The neighbors must surely know something is wrong, heck even the Vatican might have heard this alarm for all I know. The youngest child, a girl is looking around trying to make some sense of all this, tears streaming down her pudgy cheeks. The mother is staring at the pool, shaking badly, clearly in shock. I put my muzzle on my front paws watching as the scene changes from one of running and hiding for their lives to seeing what I am positive was grandma, floating in the pool with two 45 slugs in her brain.

I don't know if the alarm timed out finally or the alarm company turned it off, but mercifully it is no longer screaming at us. I can somewhat hear sirens coming up the dirt road out front. The dust, once again billowing up over the rooftop from the other side of the home can be seen even at night, is a giveaway. Liam walks around the pool to join me sitting on the small stem wall taking out his identicard indicating we are a clearing team, his pistol safely re-holstered.

Short moments pass for the local law enforcement to come spilling into and through the home and for a tense moment, with their guns drawn and yelling, things can always go sideways. Neither Liam nor I make any moves. Thankfully it seems this group of patrolmen seem to be aware of the situation. Though they approach us with caution, soon there is also a holstering of weapons and drawing out of their identipads to tag the kill to our team for payment and clearance. We aren't permitted to leave the scene until all the details are sorted out. Dead body in pool was a confirmed Myrna, yup check. Initial 911 call was made dispatching a wolf team, yup check. Everything is in order and shortly we are told to clear out while they await a Crows Nest dispatch. All the uniformed officers look relieved they don't have to do the inevitable paperwork associated with a messy dead body.

Trotting around to the front of the home and up to Liams car, pawing at the sliding side door I hit the button release. It slides open smoothly. Hopping in, Liam follows behind me until he gets into the drivers side front and buckles up. I lay down and we make the drive home. I can smell he is frustrated with me. And we'll have to have a discussion on how to get my vehicle back home as well. I sigh heavily, knowing the conversation we'll have to have soon. All the way home he broods while I catch a quick nap.

....

My mate changes back to human in our master bedroom. Females really do have an easier time of it. Their change is slicker and quicker requiring only a few minutes as opposed to males. We can take anywhere from ten to thirty minutes. No matter, it is still painful to watch the bones break and reform, skin to stretch and bleed and pop before settling back into its familiar and remembered form. Sweat is glistening off her skin, teasing my nose with it's silky musky odor that is all her.

Ellan has always hated how strong her musk is due to her change, but I adore it. I should give her a good tongue lashing for pulling such a stupid stunt. Wolves don't work alone. But somehow I don't think that will change a thing. Walking up behind her I wait patiently as she stretches out the last kinks and pains of the change. When she turns to face me, I know its safe to run my hands gently over her arms. Leaning in to inhale her scent, I let it wash over me as I nuzzle her neck and murmur "No holes? Nothing broken, mangled, or bitten?"

"Don't be silly, you'd have known by now if that was the case." Ellan snaps. "I'm fine, don't worry." She adds more gently. She's just mad because I should chastise her for being foolish enough to run off without backup, without me. But I am letting it go this time and she knows it. That doesn't change how mad and scared I was for her, but yelling at Ellan almost always ends up in me saying I'm sorry and her remaining mad for the whole next day. Sometimes it's just better to let it go.

Chapter 4
The Alpha's Request

Morning comes early. I don't sleep as well as I used to and sleeping in still feels like a luxury. After last nights late night Scottsdale escapade I was hoping to get to sleep in but not today. An knock comes to the front door bright and stupidly early. Six am. Ellan hops out of bed grabbing her pants stepping into them as she moves to the front of the house to answer the soft knock. She always wears a t-shirt to bed, usually one of mine. I follow behind her both out of less interest so much in answering a six am knock as well as taking the time to step into my jeans, which still hold the belt holster and pistol from last night.

"It's Mark – and I hope I smell coffee if he is coming this bloody early." Ellan says over her shoulder.

"Were we expecting him?" I ask.

"Not that I am aware of." Opening the front door reveals the local pack leader. I personally hate the term alpha. In this case, it's more a rule by consent kind of thing I've always felt. The Phoenix packs Alpha, Mark is basically a good guy. Younger than myself and with a decent regard for Ellan's status.

"Well good morning." I say from the few steps I am still behind Ellan by, who just taken the proffered cup of java and drinks deeply with her eyes closed.

"You'd think so wouldn't you, but not so much." Mark replies stepping past the threshold and giving me the second of three cups of good strong coffee from our favorite coffee house. He remembers those kinds of details. That is part of what makes him such a good leader. Taking a pause from her morning coffee happiness, Ellan motions him to sit in one of the overstuffed chairs in the front entry room.

"I need to speak with Ellan, and you too of course Liam." We look at each other. Ellan is dominant. Very dominant. She should have been the alpha by all rights, but that would have required dominance fights and lots of jockeying for positions and werewolves are still rather an archaic bunch. No one was really sure how well a female leader with an only mildly dominant mate would have been received. So in the interest of peace and harmony and perhaps even everyone staying alive, Ellan keeps to the background only going to pack functions when absolutely necessary. Mark became the de facto leader, but he still defers to her judgment in a lot of areas. Clearly he'd found another one this morning he felt should be run by her. At six am. Ellan simply raises her eyebrow in way of a query while continuing to sipping her coffee.

"It has come to my attention that we have a pair of wolves who are in the homeless population." Ellan stops mid sip making a surprised sound. "How is that possible? A hungry wolf is a danger to us all!"

Mark nods his head "Yes I am well aware of that. Apparently these two .... boys really.. just barely mid- teens, or so I've been told, were turned recently and in their first full shift may have killed their parents, who for whatever reason failed to teach them control or contain them.

Or maybe their parents weren't the wolf who turned them, I really don't know."

Ellan and I look at each other. She asks "So they are brothers?"

"Again, to the best of my knowledge yes. I haven't met them personally yet. This information comes to me through Bethy. She's seen them a couple of times while out hunting in her part of town." I let out the breath I didn't realize I was holding. Bethy is a sweet, exceptionally submissive wolf who Ellan brought into the pack a few year before she turned me. Rescued really. Bethy is completely loyal not only to Mark and the pack, but even more so to Ellan as well.

"So you are asking what of us?" Ellan intones.

"Well, I'd like you to go out there in team format one wolf one human and approach them. Get a feel for them. Bring them into the pack, and…" he pauses "maybe offer them a place to stay. They are kids. They'll need a strong hand and no other pack member has as large a home as you do, with the extra space plus your boys are about the same age."

Setting her coffee down with force Ellan quickly shakes her head "No. Period. No. This is not a bed and breakfast. And as you have mentioned we have our own children here, HUMAN children. What on earth makes you think I would acquiesce to this. You may be the pack's leader but you are not my alpha!" Ellan's temper and anger are causing her scent to shift rapidly into a dangerous zone and neither Mark nor I am immune to her force of will. I stay silent knowing full well both why we can't honor Mark's request and why we should. Soon our boys will have to make the attempt to change to wolf. Ellan is particularly touchy about the subject.

Mark sits a little lower in the chair not quite managing to give over control to Ellan but not challenging her either. His eye line looking at her neck rather than her face to not offer challenge.

In a quiet voice I say "Maybe we should at least meet these two and talk with them. Figure out what happened to them, when and where." Ellan stands up abruptly turning her ire on me

"Fine, make the arrangements, but they are NOT staying here. I am not taking in stray cubs to raise" and stalks out of the room. I look apologetically at Mark. Taking that as his dismissal, Mark hands over a slip of paper and stands to take his leave.

"Sorry Liam, I knew this would cause a stir. I should have warned you."

"No apologies necessary. She just doesn't want to be used as a problem solver, nor have untrained baby wolves around our sons."

"I can understand that and respect it, but I don't think anyone else could bring them into the fold quite as smoothly as her. Bethy said she felt they were fairly dominant, and I won't risk sending someone when we aren't basically guaranteed to do the job." Making his goodbyes, Mark takes his leave.

I sit here a minute longer contemplating the best way to approach my hot tempered mate. Getting up and following her scent through the house to the master bedroom I find her on the bed reading the current cop novel series she enjoys. Being a retired officer she has rather strict requirements for the kinds of novels she reads.

Ellan puts the book down and purses her lips in frustration at me. I know she's heard Mark's parting words about the kids being dominant and why he was making such a request. Wolves even in human guise, have better than average hearing making very few conversations private.

"Let's drive by, see if we can spot them and make a plan from there. It's still early." I offer. Ellan's scent is calmer now. Less musky and angry. I feel a bit more confident in making the suggestion.

"Fine but you're driving." She says getting up from the bed to finish dressing more fully.

Chapter 5
Foundlings

Driving downtown in the stop and go traffic is not a task well suited to my mate. She much prefers the wide open road where her lead foot can be given ample freedom. With the windows down, even in early spring, it's still rather warm out. Welcome to Phoenix. I enjoy driving, always have so the dynamic works well. We head east, towards the inner city area of 7th Street and Jefferson where the address Mark gave us indicates. The two boys who are suspected new wolves were last seen in that area a few days ago.

Sadly the cities streets are riddled with many homeless taking shelter by the roads side and in various empty buildings, walkways and parking areas. Phoenix is not the mecca of tech and industry it once was and downtown has suffered for it the last few decades. Some homeless can be seen talking to themselves, even arguing with their unseen inner demons. A few are still bundled up in blankets even though it is warming up very quickly and will easily reach ninety degrees today. With our windows open, it should be simple catch any indications of scent that will tell us a werewolf is in the area. Two presumably unwashed teenage werewolves shouldn't be that hard to detect even from a slowly moving vehicle.

As predicted, it's just a couple of streets further south and we find them. A pair of boys, maybe 16 at best. I pull the car over to a metered parking space and while I fuss over the right coins to use, which by the way, why are we still using coins in today's day and age I couldn't tell you but we still do, Ellan gets out and starts walking slowly towards them. So much for only scouting them. Fairly unremarkable young fellows, both with dark scraggly hair that once had some kind of style but now is just shaggy and unkempt. Dirty jeans and not quite torn tennis shoes. Stinky worn T shirts make for a picture perfect ensemble of homelessness.

Approaching with caution, Ellan calls out to them when she gets within a few feet. "Hola chicos, ¿hablan inglés?" She has raised one hand open palmed hopefully so they don't think she is a social worker. Both boys freeze and watch her warily. The taller of the two takes in a deep breath. It would seem he recognizes us as werewolves as well because he shutters his eyes, steps in front of what must be his younger brother and growls in warning.

Placing her hands on her hips Ellan, stops advancing and sighs. "You know, I was hoping this would go more smoothly." and with a small push of power she commands them "Stop that." The older boy stops so suddenly his eyes fly open, his mouth forms an O of surprise at his immediate obedience. The younger boy steps out from behind him, smiling and says "¿cómo lo hiciste?" with a thick accent.

"How I did that is because I am older and wiser than you." Ellan says. The youngsters big grin fills his face and lights his eyes.

"You gotta teach me that lady." He says.

Ellan returns the smile and replies "You gotta earn that kiddo." Sitting on the sidewalk's edge so as to appear less threatening, she pats the cement in invitation. The younger boy, already in her thrall hops over and plops himself down beside her. The older boy, more wary and still concerned moves closer none the less, not convinced this is a good plan.

"My name is Ellan and this is my mate and husband Liam. What are your names?"

"He's Ramon and I'm Isaac. Are you hungry? I'm hungry. Can we get some food?" Isaac asks. It's clear this youngster has decided Ellan is in charge and I guess she really is. After all that's why Mark sent us here the first place isn't it.

"Well Isaac we'd like you to tell us what happened to you. How did you get here? And how did you get changed? Who changed you?"

Isaac drops his eyes and the smile leaves his face. Ramon puts his hand on his brothers shoulder. "We are from Mexico. Our parents were killed. We were like this when we woke up." he says defensively. I look down into his young face. His scent is fluctuating between fear, anger, protectiveness and guilt.

"You have nothing to be afraid of from us, nor do you, I believe, have anything to be guilty of niÑos. But you can't stay out here on the streets either." Looking around making sure we aren't drawing any eyes, my mate continues "Ok, lets go get some lunch and you can tell me your tale." The brothers look at each other and back to Ellan then to me. Well, it's not as bad a reaction as I feared. They didn't turn tail and run or start yelling and drawing unwanted and unneeded attention. Their scents fluctuate a bit from fear to interest and back. Feeding a hungry werewolf is always a good way to make friends.

"Is there anything you want to bring with you?" Ellan asks. I can smell the indecision too, and she is hoping to calm them a bit so we can move forward. I am rather a more direct creature. Maybe it's the wolf in me, but I was always a hard head. "Do you have other family here in the states? Or in Mexico?" They both shake their heads. Each has a small worn backpack they take up as they trail behind us to our van, like good pups.

We take lunch at the local drive n dine style place. The girl at the window doesn't even bat an eye at our order of eight double burgers with fries and drinks. Maybe she's fed werewolves before. More likely she just doesn't care as long as the bill is paid.

As the teens gobble down what is very likely their first filling meal in a long time, they pass looks between each other indicating a discussion and determination that neither Ellan nor I are a part of. Following this, they seem content enough to let us drive them somewhere other than downtown Phoenix. Before leaving Ellan calls Mark, the Alpha of the Phoenix pack.

"Hey Mark we found your stray cubs. Tell Bethy they are safe. She did good. Liam and I will be bringing them over as soon as we finish up our lunch. No family, don't know who turned them and both boys are under 18. They can brief you more fully when we all arrive at your place." She hangs up before Mark has a chance to really protest, not that he would have put too much effort into it really. He's good like that.

Ellan takes over the driving and we get them to the Alpha's house on the north west side of the Valley. His home isn't as big as ours, but she refuses to get any more sucked into pack business. Stray's were the packs problem, not ours. Yet here we are, chauffeuring them around. I had texted Mark some additional basics of the outcome as well as including our ETA. It will be up to the Alpha now to train and guide these boys. He and Cindy, Marks' human wife don't have kids of their own, and I am pretty sure Cindy speaks Spanish. As a duly licensed lawyer and CPA she also has the resources to dig into these kids backgrounds and make sure everything is done right.

Part of an alpha's job is to train new wolves properly. But so few packs have a real alpha. We are lucky. Most packs are nothing but a bunch of dangerous frat boys with bad tempers. We have more than our share of female werewolves because of this very problem. But women, children and these boys are all safe in Marks care.

Chapter 6
Changes Are Coming

The paramedics, one driving and one in the body of the ambulance, are racing towards the nearest trauma room. Their patient is a mid twenties young woman who has severe abdominal trauma involving all the major organs. Spleen, liver, pancreas, intestines are just the start. Having been impaled by a large portion of her older cars metal body when it was hit by a freshly turned Myrna zombie driver is not a common occurrence in today's world but it happens more and more frequently as the number of Myrna's increase.

The paramedic responsible for stabilizing the car crash victim, Dell was a long time pro. Not much rattled him. The young woman the firefighters had extracted wasn't expected to survive. She had lost too much blood. It appeared as if she had been practically severed in half like some morbid magicians stage trick of sawing the lady in half, gone horribly wrong. Dell had set an IV with fluids and added morphine to ease the pain. Her blood pressure was dangerously erratic as was her heart beat. He had no idea who she was, nor did he care. Right now, his job was to keep her alive until they arrived at the level one trauma center. Holding direct and firm pressure on her abdominal cavity using the one and only package of surgifoam onboard, he was very afraid that it soon wouldn't matter. Then he'd only have to worry about how long it took her to turn into one of those zombie things and hope he had time to strap her down so she didn't kill them all.

She flutters her eyelids and gives a low moan. *Damn,* he thinks. *I wish that morphine would hold her longer.* She struggles and he leans in a bit harder trying not to dislodge the foam pad while holding her and it in place. For almost being dead, she is still fairly strong.

He wonders if she's a drug addict and that's why the morphine was less effective. She is managing to still flail her limbs now a bit more than he is comfortable with, and frowning he watches them. Unable to do anything about it. To his astonishment, her arms begin to transform before his eyes. The skin folds and stretches, while the bones underneath seem to be breaking with audible pops and visual reshaping as well. What started out as a moan becomes a canine growl as her bottom jaw elongates. Facial bones reshape, the human nose shortens to a rough pad while her cheeks begin jutting forward, to accommodate the mouth of impossible teeth.

"Shit!" Dell yells to the front "No one told me she is a werewolf!"

"What?" Lauren responds in a panic glancing back only briefly. A loose werewolf in a small ambulance space is a bad combination. Some companies even refuse to dispatch or pick up if it's known the injured is a wolf.

Yelling to the font again, Dell instructs his partner "Call dispatch, tell them to have the local Alpha meet us in the ER." He knows he has to remain calm to work on any of the wolves, but a fatally wounded wolf in the start of shifting with no alpha around; well maybe he should have retired like his wife wanted him to do.

....

My eyelids flutter open and my brain explodes with the pain. I am in an ambulance the siren so loud it overwhelms my senses and hurts. Everything hurts. It all hurts. I panic. My senses are overwhelmed. I growl trying to get my feet underneath me only noticing at this point that I'm still in my human guise. I call for the change to sweep over me but it's like I'm strangled in the pain. I can't breath, my middle is torn apart and nothing beyond my limbs listens to my call. The new push of adrenaline pumps more blood out my gaping wound, even though I can see the medic desperately attempting to stem the flow. Mercifully I black out.

·········

Forty eight hours later and Mark is still sitting in the lone uncomfortable metal and plastic chair in the hospital room of his pack mate. Jennifer is laying on the stark white linen covered bed with an IV drip in her forearm and her abdomen completely encircled in a pressure bandage held more secure with medical adhesive. As she stirs, her alpha places a reassuring hand on her arm to keep the panic from taking hold. Her eyes are open but unfocused.

"I can't breath. I can't feel my wolf. What is going on? Please help me." She pleads tears running down her face. Mark croons to her softly and Jennifer falls back into blissful unconsciousness once more. Mark sighs, he knows that soon he will have to tell her what's happened. He has already told Julia, her twin sister and she did not handle the news well. She bolted out of the room at the pronouncement and hadn't returned yet. He called Julia's working partner to let him know to keep an eye out for her. He'd hate to loose both of his wolves.

·······

I come to a few days later, slowly. My crusty eyes flutter open only upon pain of my forcing them to do so. The taste in my mouth is dusty, dry and I'm pretty sure something died recently there. Unsurprisingly Mark is still reclining in the same blue plastic and metal chair watching a rerun of Maverick. I wonder if he's been here the whole time. He looks at me and smiles.

"There you are," he says softly "You scared us." I look around the room, at my arm with an IV still attached to it, and back to Mark. He has such a kind and soft expression on his face. "Julia was here, but she left. I'm sure she'll be back soon." I hear his words, but his voice belies the lie. My Alpha continues "Are you able to talk? We need to discuss what's happened."

I try to sit up but a flash of pain causes me to gasp instead. Mark jumps up and his look changes to one of concern as he offers his hands out to help me, to do what I'm no longer sure. Mark's phone rings from his jeans pocket and he pauses to take it out. "Hang on a moment Jennifer. Ellan is calling." he says as he picks up the call. "Yes Ellan, what did you discover?..... Uh huh..... are you sure?..... Yes of course I know your source is good, I'm not implying otherwise but it really is unthinkable if true........ Let me get back with you, I am in with Jennifer just at the moment. Have Jim, my second, call a pack meeting tonight my house. I'll text Cindy so she is aware,... yes you and Liam need to both be there as well. Goodbye" He holds the phone a bit away from his face for just a moment, lost in contemplation.

Out of habit I was not trying to listen in on the conversation, but being a werewolf sometimes you can't help but overhear other peoples conversations. But then I realize it wasn't courtesy that caused me to not listen in, it was lack of ability. I simply couldn't hear the other end of the conversation that was taking place less than two feet from me. My eyes well up, my nose gets thick and giant tears spill down my face.

Mark just reaches over and hugs me. After a few minutes I manage to pull myself together enough to raise my bed to a truly sitting position. "So" he says, "I guess we need to talk."

Chapter 7
Loss And Learning

I'm not a wolf any longer. I can't shift. Mark was right. The doctors were right and I am sure I will end up in some published journal somewhere because of it. I can't hear as well as I could, I can't see as well as I could. I can't smell as well as I could. I have no job outside of killing Myrna's and I am only a liability to my partner now. I can't help him. We aren't mates or even lovers. I'm sure he will have to find a new partner quickly to keep working.

My parents kicked my sister and I out when they learned Julia and I had been turned. So no real family or education to fall back on either. I wonder if anyone has told mom. I think she'd be concerned. Is that the right word? Cindy has been great. I talked to her on the phone after Mark's revelation that I am no longer a werewolf. She's not a wolf either. She said she'd help me find a job and a place. Mark said the pack won't abandon me. I've refused all antiserums so far due to my wounds still healing so I can't or won't turn into one of the walking dead, yet. Well that's a plus. But I can't hold off forever. I know I just learned this today. But there's a pack meeting tonight, soon and I'm here in the hospital still. Not pack anymore, not really. How can I be pack, if I'm not wolf? I think Mark got an inkling of what I am thinking. I've never been overly dramatic, at least I don't think I have. But I am only half of what I was. It's like someone scooped out my core and left the shell. Which I guess from the car accident, is almost what happened. Julia ran off at the news and still hasn't answered her phone. I'm so very tired. I better do this quickly. Maybe from the roof, if I can get up there. Picking up my cell phone from the rolling tray I try Julia's cell again. Praying it goes to voice mail I listen to it ring.

After the fourth ring, her message comes on "Hi this is Julia. If you are asking about a hunt leave a message, if you are looking for Jennifer this is not her number ha ha she fooled you. And pretty much if you are anyone else, yeah good luck!" The electronic beep sounds but I hesitate, taking a deep breath I say "Hey Jule's it's me. I love you. So much." I pull the phone away from my ear and wipe my eyes with the top of my bed sheet. Hanging up, I make myself get up. I'll have to move quickly.

••••••

Mark has called the whole pack in tonight. Though not small, Mark's home or more specifically his living room wasn't designed for so many people. Twenty three pack members, with the absence of both Jennifer and Julia but with the additions of Isaac and Ramon, as well as Liam and Ellan makes for an uncomfortably tight fit. Tempers could run high with the space or lack of it, being the tipping point. Ellan is doing her best to stay out of the way in a corner with her mate Liam where no one can get behind them. She is watching the goings on, taking note of who is there and what they seem to be feeling. Like high school; alliances are made, members stick with friends and the weak stay to the edges hoping not to be noticed. She never wanted to be the center of attention but the news she has to share is too big. She'd rather know her audience than make a misstep in a pack that already doesn't seem to trust them too much.

Stepping to the center of the room Mark clears his throat in the time honored 'stop what you are doing and look at me' way. No force of will or shove of power needed. All of the members gather around taking seats or sitting on the floor in accordance with their dominance within the structure of the pack itself. A few wolves shoot furtive glances Ellan's way, but it's clear from their alpha's body language that they are welcome and accepted. Not interlopers or usurpers. This is not a coup.

"Thank you for coming on such short notice. I'm sure you have all heard about Jennifer's car accident." A murmur breaks out between those that did and those that didn't know. Mark gives it a few seconds for folks to get the information disseminated and work their nerves out. He's a very good coordinator of these types of events.

"Well today, sadly we learned something new about our natures. Apparently, it is in fact possible for enough damage to be done to our bodies to no longer be able to become the wolf." There is a general outbreak of disbelief, shock and a wave of fear that ripples through the underbelly of the emotions. Continuing on, "Obviously this is a first but once it gets out, there might be those who want to capitalize on the information. No I don't know how just yet, but we all know nefarious people do nefarious things." He pauses to let that information sink in. Taking a deep breath he continues sweeping the room making eye contact with several of the wolves ensuring their attention "More importantly right at this moment, is why Jennifer was in that car accident. We all know Myna's have a hard time functioning past a certain point of repetition or pattern, but what Ellan has learned from her Crows Nest contacts is even more disturbing." Turning to

Ellan, who is seated behind him, Mark takes a step to the side leaving the path clear for her to step forward.

"Good evening everyone. What happened to Jennifer is criminal I know. But more disturbingly is the fact that the driver that hit her, was in an advanced Myrna state. And not just any Myrna state but a drugged out or rather up condition that the government is calling A-mpd. I'm not sure if its the drug they are calling this or the state of the Myrna when given this drug. But the results are catastrophic. These things were dangerous before – they are insane now." She pauses looking around the room. Most are giving her a wide eyed stare of disbelief, a few are frozen in fear but two seem to be avoiding her gaze entirely. Ellan inhales deeply, giving every time to to process this while she susses out the room better to isolate the two her instincts are telling her something is going on with. Continuing her information "The Crows Nest just became aware of this new drug recently and thankfully it's not common, nor commonly known yet. But it's only time as we all know. An A-mpd Myrna is faster and more agile than ever before and if given the drug prior to them going full zombie their memories remain intact." This new information causes a general murmuring to fill the room as the implications are felt. Fear, anxiety and anger all ramp up to choke the air. "This is scary stuff folks. Absolutely do not attempt to take one out by yourself, work in pairs only and let others know when you run across these...well- super zombies. It's like something out of a bad movie."

Mark's second, Jim, straightens himself up in his chair and tries to make eye contact with Ellan at the implied order she's given. He's an older wolf having been turned in the 1950's so the modern age is still a bit of a mystery to him.

Mark, spotting the beginnings of a fight, steps between the two before either can take offense or elevate it any further,redirecting the room back to him with a quick motion of his hands while responding "Great advice, thank you." Jim settles back in his chair but is still showing signs of being huffy over what he perceived as an order from a wolf not in the pack. A phone rings and everyone blinks looking around wondering who left their cell phone on during a pack meeting. Mark reaches into his jeans pocket pulling his offending phone out. Holds his finger up for quiet and answers with "Hello this is Mark."

"Hi, this is Phoenix General Hospital. We need you to come down here right away please. There has been an ….incident." The voice on the other end says. Nothing like a private conversation in a room full of werewolves.

"Of course, what has happened? Is Jennifer okay?" Mark asks while hurrying towards the front door.

"I'm sorry to inform you but Jennifer Gadsdon has passed away. We can't reach her sister and you are her next Power of Attorney."

Mark hangs up the phone bolting out of the room towards his vehicle. The wolves have all heard the hospitals end of the conversation and lift their heads in a unified howl of pain and loss. Liam and Ellan join in. Cindy comes into her living room, not having heard the phone call or the cause, only knowing something has changed.

Chapter 8
The Contract

I remember our first conversation about being included as a part of the Phoenix packs contract to kill the Myrna's. Ellan was, to say the least, very reluctant. Eventually she understood the necessity of it from all the angles.

"Oh those poor people" Ellan says while busy making breakfast.

"Believe me honey, they aren't people any longer." I respond.

Turning to look at me "Oh so its okay to eat them?" Sarcasm dripping from every word. I think I hear the eye roll with that comment.

"Of course not and we don't eat them, yuck! We just crush their spinal column at their neck so they cease to be a threat. How long have you told me you want to quit your job and retire, that you hate it. This would ultimately be killing two birds with one bite!" Liam finishes with a small chortle.

"I am well aware of my options. Remember I turned you. I've been a wolf a whole lot longer than you have. But there are other implications involved. When we start hunting other humans..." She leaves off shaking her head.

"They are NOT human by any stretch of the imagination."Liam interrupts "They are vicious creatures who can kill a dozen mundane normal humans in a matter of minutes if we wolves don't step in. We perform a public service, ensure the government looks favorably on werewolves and earn a living wage without the discrimination."

"You think I am not aware of this?" She snaps. "Or haven't weighed these options? Since when did you of all people think working for the government as a good thing?" She adds, the flash in her eyes a warning.

Tilting his head head off to the side just a smidgen as a sign of deference to his mate, Liam says "You know killing these things is a good policy. And we get paid to do it. How does that hurt anyone?" A bit more softly than before. "It gives the wolf a place in society that we didn't have before."

Ellan practically tosses the bowl onto the table, her eyes alight with anger "Do you know what happens to a wolf who's been bitten by one of these things?" Not waiting for his response, she hotly continues "Well I do. I've seen it. First hand. Is that really what you want our kids to see on the news feeds?" Pausing for breath she lowers her voice but her eyes still flash in anger " I don't want to fight over this. If you want to hunt, be my guest. For now, my answer is no. Let's just have some breakfast." Ellan sets a pair of serving plates on the table top laden with bacon and eggs.

•••••••

It was just a few weeks later when in Ohio the new feeds ran graphic stories of two wolves who has been trapped and killed by an out of control group of Myrna's. The media outlets had shared with glee the blood and body parts in vivid detail. And the watchers who had stood by filming, some even laughing on camera, had soon found themselves in pools of their own intestines and blood when those same Myna's turned on them after the werewolves were dead and no longer interesting.

Nobody did anything on that day. No one seemed to care except for the sensational news it made. Ellan did. Mark did. Together they signed contracts with the Arizona State Governors Office, the state police's executive director, divisions of emergency management and even Game and Fish, who later named a sub set of their agency to become the point of contact, code named The Crows Nest.

Soon other contracts included most of the remaining counties Sheriff's offices within the very next year. It was a lot to enforce and oversee. Mark's people were stretched thin, but overall did a fantastic job. Lethal Myna attacks dropped by over sixty percent in the first two years alone.

Additional wolves moved into the territory held by Mark, joining the pack and earning a living. Discrimination was no longer as widely held a belief. And amazingly other states soon joined in, following the Phoenix Packs example. Cindy, Marks human mate, was brilliant at her job and brokered several deals for other packs in other states because of it.

We no longer had to hide in the shadows, skulking like some bad "B" movie villain, hoping to avoid detection. We became as much a part of society as any group. Even Congress has now taken notice, though none of us are sure if that's a good or bad thing. As long as we are disposing of confirmed Myrna's we are an asset to society.

Ellan and I do a lot of seek and destroy these days. It's become our thing.

Chapter 9
Our First
A-mpd Zombie

Ellan watches me stop the forward movement of my tracking and look back at her. She catches up to me the few steps while glancing ahead. She is most likely thinking I have spotted our prey. But I have stopped for another reason.

Standing by her side, I am open mouth panting and I wipe my slick muzzle on her hand. She looks down in recognition of whats going on and pulls a very dried summer sausage out of a pocket and unwraps it offering it to me. Giving it a quick chomp and swallow, I gently bump her with my shoulder as I again take the lead and continue tracking this weirdly elusive Myrna I know we both can smell.

This thing is moving fast but so far we haven't found any bodies left in its path. Sheer luck that I fear at some point will run out. We need to find this thing and bring it down. This part of the west valley isn't as populated as a few decades ago when they thought it was going to be the new Silicon Valley. But there are still plenty of empty warehouses and burned out areas to search through.

The heat is bothering me more than I thought. June in Arizona is hot. The Crow's Nest has sent us out after what they believe to be a new A-mpd Myrna. They can do a lot more damage than traditional ones. They are faster and stronger with some basic reflexes regular Myrna zombies don't have. Isn't that a great thought.

This one seems to be meandering more than rampaging. Nothing to stimulate it I guess. I pick up the pace as its scent trail gets stronger. Ellan isn't far behind me but human legs can't travel as fast as a wolf on four feet. I quickly outdistance her without noticing it.

Turning a corner I find myself in a blind driveway. This was built as a tractor trailer turn around point but now is only cluttered with tumbleweeds, plastic bottles and other human waste and debris. I can see the Myrna has essentially trapped himself there. He is still blissfully unaware that he is in a dead end and continues to try pushing himself through a particularly large and nasty tumbleweed that takes its own sort of revenge by pricking tiny black oozing holes all over this things bare chest and arms while catching and tearing his dirty pants. My wolf is excited to find its prey and picks up speed. My ears prick forward while my brain fuzzes over into it's more predatory space.

Recklessly, I launch myself at the Myrna, whose back is to me. Somehow the thing hears me and turns around at the last second. Subsequently, I have misjudged my leap. I sail a bit past the neck and land badly, barely managing to miss the huge tumbleweed. Both hind legs go out from underneath me and I land hard on my hip, sliding a bit with the force of my leap. The impact jars my bones and I am aware of a deep sensation of something not being quite right in my left rear hock. My human thoughts come flooding back at the awareness of the pain. The killing brain fuzz cleared now to leave me very concerned.

Normal wolves are fast. Werewolves tend to be a bit faster, but for some reason this Myrna was pretty darn fast too. And then the fight started in earnest.

Silent from my aspect, wolves learned long ago to be silent during a hunt and I am no exception. I allow my wild brain to lead me in all the right directions and best positions. Myrna's however are like ......I don't know what. For being dead they make the most extreme of sounds. High pitched shrieks, grunts, cries, wails and more. Get two or more of them together and it can deafen a wolf for a short period of time, eventually limiting the use of their ears if the fight becomes prolonged.

There is nothing human left of a Myrna, and this one was no exception. They are blood and bone and tissue but the body is deceased, the heart doesn't beat but the stubborn brain refuses to stop sending signals. I remember performing the experiment of putting salt on frogs legs in high school science class to make them twitch. Yup that's usually about what you are facing. Basic survival signals are to kill and eat. And no pain. They feel nothing. You can disable a limb but it doesn't even slow them down. Mostly. But this thing was now rapidly advancing on me more quickly than I had ever seen one do so before, in an attempt to rend me into many tiny pieces. For a preternatural creature this thing is fast and agile. I have to scramble to get out of its way but I am limping now and not as agile from that rear leg refusing to support my weight. Add to that, smooth cement floors suck for traction.

Being in human guise my mate had to take the long way around and hasn't met up with us yet. *Where is she?* I think *I could be in real trouble here!* I am sure she's close and coming. Her hearing would have told her there was a problem. She is carrying the water, food and right now more importantly, her revolver.

The dead thing lunges at me, close enough to see its no longer comprehending eyes. I dodge to the side ducking under its wild grab. We do this lunge, dodge and turn step dance a few times, neither gaining any advantage. My sprained hock is keeping me from effectively doing more than staying out of clawing and biting range of this thing.

I hear my mate coming but can't spare a moment to look in her direction.. *"Down, down now"* I hear her command in my head. Her order comes to me from pushing her wolfs dominant force of will. I immediately drop to the ground as if my legs were no more than jello. My wolf trusts her implicitly, but I also follow the command instinctively of a substantially more dominant wolf.

I feel the push of air before the roar of sound as three 357 slugs come slamming past me, over my head, now as flat as I can get on the hot cement. The first two shots hit mid chest, the force causing the Myrna to stagger backwards several steps but somehow it remains upright until the third shot penetrates it squarely between the eyes. It pauses a second or two, as if contemplating its sudden final demise. Then crumpling into an inert stinking heap it finally stops moving. Ellan only stops running when she reaches me, flinging herself to the ground at my side running her hands over my muzzle, sides and body feeling for bites or wounds that would indicate I am about to become a very dangerous out of control werewolf. Her hands are soft but firm, making sure I am not seriously injured. Out of her pocket she gives me another dried large piece of beef to be sure I don't burn out. Trust her to have something like that in her pocket, and I realize I am indeed hungry. My body was burning calories like crazy to maintain its thermodynamics. Unfortunately the Arizona heat causes us to burn more calories to keep our bodies at a normal and safe temperature. We pant more, our noses drip sweat, and its possible to even lose traction as I have discovered on our feet from the excess sweat. Most likely the cause of my earlier fall.

Ideal werewolf weather is basically Southern California. Anything too far above or below the mid ranges and we start burning calories like a wildfire. And we need fuel to counter this in the form of food. Some lesser wolves who can't fuel their burn look drunk, unable to function and eventually fall into a stupor to die if not assisted. Those wolves who are more dominant during a fuel burn get hangry. Remember those old candy bar commercials where the people get mad and aggressive when hungry – yup that's a dominant wolf only with a mouth full of teeth. Seems a rather innocuous name for such a huge problem that can end up almost as bad a Myrna rampage. Hangry wolves can turn on innocent mundanes, law enforcement, their own teams, pretty much anyone. Those wolves will recover after killing and eating sufficient quantities of protein or being captured and force fed through restraint. Of course, being killed works too. There is a story that all wolves are told about one such occurrence when a wolf lost control on an extended hunt and ended up in such a state. He is said to have killed his mate before being subdued by pack members and force fed into recovery. Eventually returning to his human form the poor fellow committed suicide by silver bullet. I would really not like to end up as a cautionary tale, so I am pleased and smack my lips while nuzzling my mate to signal things are under control. Who would have guessed how fragile we wolves really can be. Ellan gives a slow once over again and pulls out her phone contacting the Crows Nest about the kill. Then we wait.

Chapter 10
Permission Granted

Mark shakes his head. "Are you kidding me? Are you trying to get me killed? You do know who your mother is right?" he asks incredulously.

Both boys, Jack and Patrick, have come to his home to ask him to turn them. To make them werewolves before the government steps in and forces them either out of the country for non-compliance or captures them for the injected serum regime. And they've made convincing arguments to be sure. The odds said they would both have the requisite vestigial organs necessary to complete the DNA activation that occurs when a person is so severely mauled they would otherwise die. Some scientists call it an extreme example of the Recapitulation Theory as well as an apparent ability to consciously control our Hox genes.

Mark was no scientist but felt it was as good an explanation as any. However, if their own parents hadn't turned them already, or made the offer to by now, he wasn't sure he wanted to get involved. Marks wife Cindy brings some lemonade into the living room for them. She is not a werewolf, and looks on with concern at her husband, but leaves them to their conversation, trusting in his judgment. Even though he is the Alpha of The Phoenix Pack, oddly enough he isn't the most dominant wolf in the territory. Jack and Patrick's mother hold that dubious honor. She declined the role of alpha and subsequently isn't even a pack member, feeling it would cause too many fights and sides to be chosen.

Mark appreciates her concern for both the pack and her own family. The problem is, both her boys are adults now. Eighteen and twenty and if they weren't going to be turned, then by government mandate would have to start citizenship service by age twenty one or face incarceration, forced deportation or forced into conscription and with each of those options regardless, came the required antiserums that were now proven to cause the Myrna zombie status of some. They had put him in a tough position.

The kitchen door opens. Both Ramon and Isaac come tripping in, pushing and shoving each other and bringing the playful loud noise that is their signature with them. They have become wards of Mark and Cindy blending in well to their new lives. Catching a whiff of the tensions in the air both boys halt mid shove and look from Jack and Patrick to Mark. The four boys know and like one another having gone out to the movies a few times and just hanging out.

"Hi boys, Cindy's in the kitchen, take your homework in there," Mark directs. Once more, glancing furtively between the two factions, Ramon and Isaac leave the room more subdued than when they had entered.

"If you won't change us, then we'll go to Utah or even try the Los Angeles pack, but you know how that will look. I hear there is still a formal Montana pack too" Patrick tells Mark. "I am out of time. I turn twenty-one soon and then what?"

Sighing heavily Marks responds "And you know your mother could kill me, my wife and most of the pack over this." Patrick rolls his eyes. It's disconcerting how much he looks like Ellan when he does that.

"Fine. I'll do it. BUT my condition is you call your mother and tell her specifically this conversation here and now. No surprises, no waffling."

Jack pulls out his phone and makes the call. The ensuing conversation is short. More surprisingly there is no screaming, cursing or death threats. Mark can hear both ends of the conversation and is very well aware that Ellan knows he is standing in the same room. Being a werewolf can make having private conversations difficult, but for this conversation he needs to know everyone is on the same page and that there won't be any overt repercussions or retribution. Mark knows just how strong Ellan's wolf is even if her children don't yet. And while respecting her decision to stay out of the pack is what permits him to lead, these are still her children.

Jack ends the call with "I know mother and I love you, but we both know this has to be done."

From the other end of the line Ellan returns, knowing Mark can hear her, "Mark, make sure I don't bury my sons today". The line goes dead. Cindy comes back into the room. Softly she puts a hand on Marks shoulder looking up at him questioning the decision that has been made. She is the only one in the house who was unable to hear Ellan's end of the conversation. Placing his hand over hers he gives her an affectionate kiss to the top of her head. Breathing in her unique scent of shampoos, soaps, office carpet and the slight musk that is his human mate. He looks her in the eye "Don't worry. We're good". Nodding, Cindy returns to the two mostly adopted teen werewolves in the kitchen currently making a passable attempt at doing their homework and pretending to not catch bits and pieces of the drama playing out.

"Okay boys, lets go. I am not bloodying up my yard."

Chapter 11
Jack's Change

Piling into my large passenger van is easier and safer than either of the boys taking one or both of their cars. If Patrick and Jack make the transition to wolf successfully, they will be on four paws for at least the next twenty four hours. Then again, if they don't, my large van can be used to haul the bodies back to their parents. I can call the Crows Nest to come out and formally ID the bodies as failed changings, but not before letting Ellan and Liam say their goodbyes.

Failed changings are not considered murder nor punishable under current contract law; and the phone call ensures that aspect of my wife's safety, should the unthinkable happen. The pack would get charged a clean up fee from the government but that wasn't even on my list of concerns. My pack, thanks to my wife, was very financially stable.

The drive out to the reclaimed land designated as habitat recovery was only about thirty minutes. The Greater Phoenix area sometime in the late 2020's had radically decided that any land outside the immediate "basin" was no long permitted to be housing, business or anything else habitable. Water was at a premium and the population had shifted too much. Water rationing had come fast and hard along with new laws restricting where people could live. Entire communities had been shut down, bought out, or refused zoning. Golf clubs or anyone else with man made lakes were mandated to fill them in with xeriscaping.

Those residents with pools in private homes had to be grandfathered in with permits or filled in.

But the habitat recovery areas were still easily accessible and the Phoenix pack often used the extensive areas for monthly running on four feet. The wildlife had had a resurgence due to the lack of human interference and the pack found good hunting in some areas that satisfied their wolves need to kill. Being a civilized wolf took work and this was a way to satisfy the uglier urges. One of the many reasons Mark and Cindy had designed and drawn up the government contract to kill Myrna's.

Parking the large van at the end of the paved road where the sign indicates the demarcation to begin, the three make their way out. Handing each of the boys a small cooler I inform them "This has water and some dehydrated beef. After the change you will be hungry and this will help you gain control faster. I will change once we go a sufficient way off the main trail and then we can begin."

Neither Jack nor Patrick comment. Both know either they will die shortly, or become a preternatural creature.

The walk is short. Nerves are starting to show now that the time is at hand and I can smell both the boys anxiety and worry along with a certain amount of resignation. We reach a good location, well out of sight from the road, behind some crumbling walls able to afford us not only privacy but partly a way of more easily containing a pair of new wolves who may seek to run or fight out of confusion from the first change.

"I can't make this any easier on you. It will hurt. A lot. More than anything you have ever experienced. One of you pick who goes first and the other, I want you out of sight behind another wall. You do not need to see this." I look from one to the other. Jack nods and begins taking off his clothes. Patrick though older, turns to go around the brick wall to sit and wait. I watch him go not really thinking about the order of this, then strip down as well, folding my cloths neatly and setting them aside. Beginning my change I let it flow throw and around me. I have always found it painful but if not forced, it is not debilitating either. I had long ago gotten over any discomfiture of changing or being naked in front of others. My wolf is not one to be vicious or looking for a fight when coming out of the change so I rarely feel the need to hide, other than out of a strictly human imposed modesty.

The shivery icy hot pain slides down my spine first, spreading quickly into my bones but I keep from making any noise both from experience that the wolf knows; as well as not wanting to further scare or upset either boy. For the first moments after the change my thoughts are more wolf and instinct than man or thought. But control comes easily from practice and soon I am standing on all four paws, having shaken off the last tingles and aches.

Jack is standing naked not six feet from my wolf, with a wide stance and braced. I remember he was a wrestler all through high school and it shows in how he carries himself. Stalking up to him in a fluid motion without pause or hesitation I pounce on him knocking him onto his back on the dry ground with my claws and teeth easily rending flesh. The neck first, a quick bite and tear and red spurts as if a fountain. Jack instinctively fights back going for a punch and shove but being prepared I slide easily under both arms and rend the soft belly open before stepping backing off of him.

Trying for a roll Jack tries to come to his knees. His life blood is leaking faster and he fails, collapsing back onto the ground. Jack is weakened from the fountain of blood rapidly ending his consciousness, then soon his life. I dodge in biting hands, arms and ribs making sure to spread my affliction deeply and evenly. A single bite for some reason doesn't activate the DNA change. A mauling ensures that if the change can occur, it will. Dancing back from the fallen body and growing puddle of life's vital fluids; now it's only a matter of waiting.

•••••

The change starts as a rip through the tail bone. The vestigial portions of the body remember, through rDNA, what it once was in the womb and becomes that again at an astonishing speed. All humans have a tail around five to six weeks in the womb only to soon have it fuse into and become the coccyx or what is called the tail bone. More apropos than they know. But the six to ten bones still exist within all human bodies. And for those whose bones don't completely fuse it become the coccyx. These few have the potential to become werewolves. All the vestigial organs in your body combine to hold inactive sleeping DNA.

Body hair is one such vestigial portion. It can raise like the hackles of a dog or cat when the brain feels the need, yet people can not cause it to grow. Stress can make it turn gray or even fall out. Both within and without our control. Turning into a wolf just puts it more in our control than non-wolves. Sinuses in the cheekbones help elongate the flesh and allow the wolf's nose to form properly. Wisdom teeth it is believed help lend calcium and tooth formation as wolves like all adult dogs have 42 teeth compared to a humans 32. Maybe it has to do with extra lateral teeth, I don't know. No I don't know how that one works exactly. Undeveloped muscles in the ears blossom and find new purpose when in wolf form, allowing for full ear movement as any other canine's would. Then of course there is the appendix, which is not present in canines, but must be present in a human in order to be able to transform into a werewolf. Not all people have all of these things in their bodies and as such could never become a wolf. This is what makes becoming a wolf so dangerous. It's generally considered forbidden to try to change someone just because they ask or desire it. Could you imagine changing someone like Jeffrey Dahmer into a werewolf? Not a good game plan. As packs form, most alphas have rules and that's almost always on the top of the list. No new wolves without the alpha's knowledge and approval. That second part being required by most.

I can see the change taking hold, starting at the base of the spine and ripping Jack's body apart only to reform. Bones bend then break and reform all in a matter of minutes. Skin pops and undulates, hair becomes fur. Sometimes blood or fluids can be found from the violence of the change. When it happens to me, I just power my way through it and let the wolf's mind protect me. Watching it now happening for the first time to a young man I care about and quite frankly am a bit in fear of his mother's predominancy causes me to squirm a bit.

Stress and pain cause a newly shifted wolf to be a dangerous creature for a prolonged minute or two while they adjust. The world view changes as Jack's new vision aligns with his other senses. Cones became rods in his eyes so while he lost some of his color awareness, such as grass greens no longer being perceptible, a vast new world of gray's and blue yellows with enhanced night vision as well as motion sensing capabilities expand. The hearing greatly expands and Jack can now hear things he didn't even know were there, going from a mere 20,000hz up to an astounding 60,00hz or more. And all of these changes are immensely painful and time consuming. Females, they tell me, tend to change in a matter of two to three minutes while males can take as long as twenty or more. No one really knows why for sure, but what's been hypothesized is this reduces the stress on a females body. A few, a very few have been able to carry a human fetus to term even after a change. Dominant wolves change more quickly than lesser wolves.

If you weighed one hundred and fifty pounds as a human you still weigh that as a wolf. Jack was going to be a big wolf. His wrestling weight was let's just say heavyweight. Even if you are an obese human say north of three hundred pounds, your wolf form is much better able to manage that weight on four paws as compared to two feet. But Jack was a young man and well muscled. His wolf would be as well.

I watch as his limbs begin to retract, the bones reorganizing, breaking and shifting while nails and fur grow. I am quite sure the pain of his death was nothing as compared to this fire raging thru every organ, every nerve, every vein of his body. I can hear the blood pounding throughout his body as his heart pumps furiously to help things knit back together, pull apart again and find new ways to reform. A scream of pain begins in Jack's human throat only to have a second and stronger presence in his head stop it; warning him that sounds, screams and acknowledgment of pain are dangerous and bring other predators. Letting others know your weakness was a mistake that could be fatal. I can see Jack bite his tongue, literally and continue his change in virtual silence with only an occasional grunt or low whine. His wolf finally appears and is complete not a full thirty minutes from the time of my first attacking leap.

Weak and shaky as a newborn colt Jacks wolf stands on four feet for the first time. I can see they are learning about one another in their head when he tilts it to the side listening to his new inner voice for the first time in an inward reflection.

Chapter 12
Patricks Change

I get up from where I had been laying in the shade to wait and walk cautiously up to Jack. Not quite nose to nose but close enough. Jack raises his head and plants his feet looking me in the eyes. My wolf wants to take offense to the aggressive stance, but then realizes what it is he is seeing. Jack is more dominant than I am. Maybe not as dominant as his mother Ellan, but without her here to compare it's a close race. I lower my head and take a side step to turn to my open cooler. I retrieve the large piece of beef from within it. I drop it a few feet from Jacks still wobbly wolf. Eating always calms an unsettled wolf.

The rich scent of fresh blood, not his own, causes Jack to look down and begin salivating. Having broken the eye contact, he grabs the meat and gulps it down quickly. I wait for Jack to finish before approaching but then walk up to him again, this time with the intent to have him go back to the van as predetermined. Jack easily takes his queue reading my body language easily, and heads off in the direction of the van after making a quick pass by Patrick to assure him he is well.

Some wolves cry at the pain, some panic and flee having to be chased down and others go on the attack. Jack seems to have been born into his skin. I don't want to give that too much thought.

......

Patrick looks astounded. He heard nothing and had followed Marks suggestion of not looking. He had thought the change was more violent and noisy. Maybe it won't be so bad. Maybe his parents had been needlessly overprotective. Jacks wolf has walked by him giving him a quick sniff over while rubbing his body full length across his bent knees. He is tall and leggy, his almost coal black coat only broken by the similar white slash blazing down his face, like their fathers. Patrick watches him take off in the direction of the van as predetermined. Knowing it's his turn, Patrick gets up off the dusty ground and makes his way around the corner of the wall only to see all the fresh blood and clear fluids that haven't yet had a chance to dry and blanches. The fly's are having a lovely mid morning feast with the amount of liquid spewed in the area. Closing his eyes and swallowing hard, Patrick enters the small enclosed square that is what used to be someone's back yard and undresses, setting his clothes alongside his brothers. The stink of his fear has grown and to a new wolf such as Jack, I worry he could lose control if he were in the immediate area.

Changing someone takes control. Control to do the damage needed while not eating your victim or doing too much damage that the body can't heal from. Not all wolves have the control needed or the innate sense of what is and is not enough. This can be how some people end up dead during an attempted turning or others if attacked, can be turned unintentionally. Patrick stands as if at attention, naked with his head tilted back and his eyes closed. Feeling his fear, I move in quickly before he can change his mind. Knocking him to the ground in the same manner as Jack, I tear a large hole through his internal jugular to kill him quickly. Lying down speeds up this process as well. It's important to make it as quick as possible, should his body refuse the change the last thing I need are his remains to stink of fear and pain. Regardless of how Ellan sees this task, I do believe she would kill me for it. Funny how with Jack, these thoughts never crossed my mind. Jack's transition could not have been more smooth. For some reason I am anxious about Patrick's change so I quickly begin the grim task of partially disemboweling him, chewing on an ear and generally making him look like what law enforcement would call "attacked by animals." Finishing the task at hand I again step off the body and out of the way.

Soon enough I can see things changing and hear bones breaking but his change, unlike his brothers is slow and painful to watch. The sounds he is making are akin to screams cut off with gurgling and guttural cries. As internal structures refit themselves into differently shaped body cavities, whines and whimpers escape Patrick's newly reshaping muzzle.

Without a watch I can't be sure but it is close to the hour mark before Patrick is on his feet as a werewolf. Wobbly, shaking, head held low while he sucks in large amounts of air to allow himself to stay conscious. His wolf is tall but then in his human guise he is over six feet so that is to be expected. The tans and grays will allow him to blend into the Arizona desert very well. A white tip to his tail reminds me of the white tip on his dads tail but his muzzle doesn't have the white lightning zig zag. I walk up to Patrick and eye him easily into submission giving his wolf the body language to follow me. His head still isn't in his human thoughts and with the wolf in ascendance he easily follows a more dominant's lead and orders. Together we make our way slowly back to the van where Jack awaits us, after picking up our folded and bagged clothing in my jaws.

·····

Shortly, we arrive back at my van together, where I had instructed Jack to return to earlier. I can smell the other pair of wolves now in attendance before I see them. This could be disastrous with new wolves, who generally from the pain and fear want to fight everything. As we get closer I can identify through scent it's Liam and Ellan who are awaiting our arrival laying down in the van with their younger son, all one big happy family, or so I hope.

Patrick stops his forward motion and whines lowering his head and plastering his ears back. Wagging his tail in supplication to his parents, he bellys up to them. It's good he is received by all three with yips of welcome and muzzle cleaning. Well that's one hurdle down. Looks like no one's going to kill anyone today. At least I hope that's the case. I too had stopped, but a bit further back, to let this little greeting unfold.

Ellan hops out of the van and walks up to me not quite stiff legged but her tail held still. I stand my ground but avert my eye line, turning my head slightly. She gently grabs my muzzle to quickly release it in a soft but well meaning chiding. I'm not entirely sure why I am being reprimanded like a wayward child, but it's much better than the fight I feared. Ellan bounds off towards the open desert, and we all follow suit to begin the boys first game of chase, learning how to be a wolf.

Chapter 13
Safety Offered

Scratch, scratch scratch.............scratch scratch scratch...... breaks through my subconscious and startled, I bolt awake sitting up-right. It takes another couple of seconds for my half asleep conscious-ness to catch up.

I slide out of bed, leaving Liam asleep. These days in either form, he tends to sleep heavily. The gentle scratching is coming from our back patio's metal screen door. The security flood lights have failed to detect her motion and so it is still dark. None the less I know who is at my proverbial back door. Bethy, in her wolf form.

She always comes here when she has a bad hunt. Her given territory is the Phoenix downtown area. She and her partner Yuri, who is not her mate, look among the homeless population. Sadly they are some of the most vulnerable. No one cares too much when they die leaving the bodies to reanimate before authorities become aware. Because of this, they end up turning from simple Myrna to full zombie and then in return kill others, sometimes a lot of others, without anyone realizing or raising an alarm. But we wolves care. And Bethy cares. Mark's pack cares. Not just because its our job, which it is and we get paid well for, but to protect. We wolves are a wonderful mass of mixed bag of emotions. But a strong one, especially among females, is to protect those who need it most. And Bethy, though lowest in the packs dominance structure, is a strong protector and a surprisingly vicious little fighter. I guess you had to be to survive in her status. I don't know her whole story, some day I'll have to ask.

Tonight was one of those bad nights. One where, from the smell of her, she had discovered a child who had died and been left to turn Myna then zombie. I can still smell the mixture of undeveloped body odor from an immature human, female by the scent. Hormones barely even beginning to burgeon.

Anytime she has to put down a child, she comes here for a while. I don't really know why. I can only imagine it's some past trauma. Maybe because I am the one who found her and in some small way rescued her. Maybe because of my dominance she feels safer here. Liam has never objected. He has such a soft heart. We don't tell Mark. It would make him feel bad. It just is what it is I guess.

I open the security door and she slinks in. Her muzzle is only lightly sprinkled in the typical gore, attesting further to the diminutive size of her kill. She goes to her usual resting spot between the couch and the fireplace in the main room. Turning around twice she lays down settling her nose between her tail becoming as unnoticeable as she can on the brown and tan carpeting in the deep shadows of night. I softly close the doors and soundlessly make my way to our guest bathroom, partially filling the tub with fresh water. She'll clean herself off at some point. I keep a pair of clothes in the towel cupboard for her. Sometimes it will be months between visits. Sometimes days. Originally Liam had suggested our separate casita in the back would be quieter for her, but I don't think it's quiet so much as normal and safety she requires. We wolves, like our wild brethren, need one another. Need pack to feel truly safe and psychologically fulfilled.

I go back to bed, closing the door to our en suite for our privacy. Liam rolls over without opening his eyes "Bethy?" he mumbles.

"Bethy" I respond. He rolls back over. It takes me just a moment longer to fall back asleep.

Chapter 14
Bethy's Introduction

It's only been about a few years since I was changed. I am so restless I need to get out and run on all four feet rather than this day to day work home sleep routine. Even the baby fails to help me settle down. I have heard through the internet social sites that several of the more organized packs have group hunts on a regular basis and that is appealing to me. Liam is human and doesn't understand that itch at the back of my neck. That it becomes an incessant driving force at times to shift and run with others of my kind. Before being changed I was always a rather vocal and volatile creature. Since the change, it's gotten much worse. If I get out and run on four paws, it's much easier to control my temper. But I can't just up and leave my baby, my family or my job.

I have been hunting with Mark and the burgeoning Phoenix Pack a few times. He's the local dominant who is forming a small pack here in the Phoenix area. Thankfully he hasn't felt the need to challenge me outright because my wolfs instincts wouldn't permit that. And he's basically a good guy. It would be a shame to have kill him in a challenge. I think he could do a lot of good for werewolves in general. Also, I like both him and his human wife Cindy.

Mark has this grand idea that we wolves can not only live together but work to eradicate these damn Myrna zombie things. Right now the government is still mostly denying their existence or rounding them up. Somehow one seems incongruous with the other, but nobody asked me. I'll let him handle all of that. I'm not really a people person. Since he clearly has more savvy in that area, he's been working to get a government contract of some sort in place. In any case, I have contacted the Utah pack about coming up for a hunt and they seem pretty okay with it.

Not every group would welcome a stranger into their self-described territory, so I am planning to leave a couple of days before the full moon to drive up there. It doesn't seem like a bad trip, GPS says nine hours give or take. Mark thinks it will be good for me. He's been a wolf for quite a number of years now. He feels learning how others do things and mange is a must. I'll admit I am curious about other wolves since I haven't met many. And those I have met seem more like a gang of thugs than real people anymore. As if becoming a wolf somehow gives them leave to behave outwardly like the animal they become. The tales I have heard don't leave a good impression either. Wolves who kill, harass and bully indiscriminately and act like a bunch of frat boys rather than a cohesive pack like our wild brethren. I spent a few days short of three weeks with the so- called Angel pack soon after I was turned. They are out of Los Angeles. Let's just say there is nothing angelic about them.

Now however, Gene of the Rock Springs pack said it was fine to come up for a few days, and he would permit me to run with them. They are up in the Provo area. I am packing to leave. Not taking much, just about a weeks worth of clothes and some emergency supplies should I break down. My old four wheeler is a great vehicle that loves the open road about as much as I do. She's got over two hundred thousand miles on her and still going strong. I feel an affinity for the old machine. Together we head out, me kissing my husband and promising a swift return.

The drive up is uneventful and Mark was right. Gene and his small pack are fairly welcoming after a few bristling and pointed comments about intruders and hostile takeovers. My eye roll was strong with that one. But essentially Gene has a small stable well adjusted pack that seems to operate fairly efficiently. I think Mark is right, maybe it can be done. Maybe the key is to limit the number of pack members but then what do you do with those who want to join later? Well I am glad once again I am not the Alpha. I really dislike being in a position of authority after so many years in law enforcement. I'd rather just sit back and watch. I was always an aggressive officer, first in kind of thing. I retired when I found out I was pregnant. My husband however, is an amazing man who seems to take everything in stride. Liam even adjusted to my being turned wolf as if it happens every day.

Heading home after a great run is like the mellow after a buzz and I'm day dreaming, not really paying attention to the road ahead, heading home to my family. Whipping my mind back to my driving as a red gold streak darts across the highway ahead of me, I see she is quickly followed by the much larger forms of three what could only be werewolves based on their size. I slow my speed considerably to watch what is going on and the three larger wolves seem to have decided the little red gold streak is their prey. They are herding her in such a way as to keep her always circling and looking to her back and sides. Something about this doesn't sit right. She is too large to be a fox or even a coyote. Sadly, while I don't agree with it, they are fair game to most werewolves. Maybe she is a coydog.

Coydogs are the offspring between a domestic dog and a coyote but she looks to weigh 75 pounds or so and that's on the large side even for them. I slow my vehicle further and pull over to the shoulder of the road still keeping an eye on the chase. She is weaving back and forth intentionally crossing the highway, either as a distraction or hoping to dissuade her pursuers. Every now and then however, one of the aggressive trio is able to get close enough to take a more than just a nip at her, giving her a fresh burst of speed temporarily. But it is evident she is wearing down. There are several bloody patches on her haunches that I can spot even from this great a distance away. Slowing to a stop, I draw in a deep breath through my nose and close my eyes allowing my inner wolf to utilize her superior knowledge of cataloging and organizing scents to confirm that all four individual animals involved out there are werewolves. And I now know I have never run across any of them previously. That in itself is not odd. I'm not sure how far Gene's pack considers their territory and I know very few werewolves outside of Arizona or my short sojourn to the Angel pack. That left such a bad taste in my mouth, I decided then and there not to associate with my so called brethren.

The three larger wolves have now succeeded in trapping and surrounding the little red gold wolf. With her tail tucked under her belly and her back curled to help protect her vulnerable soft underside she is whipping her head around trying to keep all of her pursuers in sight. It's obvious these bullies were not just interested in proving dominance but rather terrorizing. Her size would have made her vulnerable in any pack but it's clear to me she's in trouble. How I could possibly know this diminutive wolf is female was brought to me by the various scent markers in the air. Her terror and panic as distinct as the beautiful blood-stained coat that could almost shimmer in the early morning of the Kanab landscape were it not for the saliva ridden tears.

These wolves were not a part of Gene's pack that I had been made aware of and my inner wolf has decided its time to stop this here and now with a low growl coming from my human throat. I hoped she could hold out while I shifted, which even at my fastest would still take several minutes. I strip while beginning my shift but when the little wolf gave a sharp Ki-yi from a pair of teeth doing more than just nipping her hind quarters I push my change as fast as I knew how. The smell of her fear and panic washes over the others raising their joy and excitement. They run around her in joy, the air a miasma of scents my wolf interprets easily.

It's more painful, the faster I change, but my anger was spurring me on. The more I hurt, the madder I get. And I was plenty mad by now. Wolves are the same weight in either form and I was a big and tall gal. The size of the red gold wolf told me this was either a child (I didn't know children could be turned, and that in itself infuriates me further) or a very small person probably no bigger than five foot and certainly no heavier than ninety-five pounds or so.

My change complete, I take a brief moment to shake off the final tingles of nerves finding new pathways and the neuropathic pain associated with that, then leap to the little wolf's aid. Racing into the fray, I intentionally give a vicious slash with my fangs to one of the bullies haunches slicing all the way to the bone in passing. His leg gives out while he bleeds copiously. His startled yelp reinforces that he hadn't noticed me or more likely felt I wasn't a threat. Does no good to have amazing senses if you don't use them. He is taken completely by surprise, as are his pack mates since none of them were paying the slightest bit of attention to me.

I rush past the aggressive trio and center myself standing over the poor little scared girl whose tail is raising dust from the ground as she wags it further seeking submission. Only then do I notice she doesn't have a couple of open nipped skin tears but rather dozens of them all over her starting from her neck, to her shoulders to her ribs to her haunches. Her fur is a mess of blood and flaps of skin. My growl, upon seeing her condition, rumbles through my entire chest and my power wildly fluctuates out of control.

The little wolf at first, being unsure if I am too out of control to not join in and become a new tormentor here to finish the job the others began, cries out piteously lowering herself all the way to the ground not quite exposing her soft under belly but laying her head to the side in desperate supplication. Her whines call to my heart. I easily tower over her placing all four feet around her, my body above hers. With my head lowered and ears pinned, my muzzle ripples with the chest deep snarl getting louder. The wolf I hamstrung moments ago is limping on three legs hanging back but still has some fight left in him. This trio appear to be a loose pack working together. I don't care, this is done. Now. The lighter colored of the three wolves has more obvious charisma and seems to be directing the other two acting as their Alpha. He lunges in, in an attempt to drive me off. I grab the side of his face and shake my head once violently ripping his cheek having never moved from my stance of protection. Startled that I didn't dodge or side step to avoid his lunge, he runs into my snapping teeth easily then yanks himself back, further tearing his face to get out of my grip. I hold my ground with his bloody skin flap in my teeth. His fresh red blood leaves a trail between the two of us. The remaining uninjured wolf looks uncertainly between the lighter wolf and myself. This second wolf takes two steps back and whines at his Alpha who turns and bites rapidly in a couple quick snaps at him in anger and frustration.

The limping wolf lunges into my shoulder attempting to disable me as I have disabled him. But he is slow and I am mad. Meeting my eyes momentarily was a mistake. I pull my force of will and dominance around me like a cloak and order him to **STOP**. Mid lunge his feet just cease moving in order to obey my command from within his brain. His momentum plants him chest firmly into the soft dirt, his muzzle turning away from me offering his soft unprotected throat in a silent entreaty. **STAY** I add to the order.

Returning my gaze to the now squabbling pair of attackers, I see the uninjured wolf has had enough and is hastily retreating back to wherever he came from. The leader of this ill conceived group is dancing back and forth on his front feet, cheek still open and dripping the bright red life's blood, but his tail is lowered and his shoulders are rolled back ready to follow his companion and flee. I've never tried controlling more than one wolf at a time. I am still fairly new to all of this, but I take a single step forward still snarling with my eye teeth exposed at this impudent ill mannered animal and he too decides to retreat to whence he came. Most of the damage done to his cheek should heal up with his next shift. Might leave a scar, but that will only serve as a reminder to behave better.

Looking down at the little red gold wolf still under me I give her a couple of gentle licks to her muzzle in reassurance. Turning my attention to the last of the offending trio I let him feel my ire at his behavior. At a further attempt at placation he wags his tail and scuttles his body on the ground not really moving forward just showing submission. Tipping my head in the direction of his comrades, he gets the message to follow them and takes off awkwardly on his remaining good three legs. His rear leg not functioning or weight bearing nor will it for quite some time. Even after a change back to human seeming that kind of damage will never fully heal. I watch them go for a good distance before turning my attention back to the small she wolf under me.

Stepping away from my self appointed charge, I motion my head toward my vehicle parked on the side of the road a short way away. Body language is easier to read and understand in wolf form and she stands up shaking herself off following me readily. Once to the vehicle I inhale deeply to be sure our nasty aggressors are well and truly gone and haven't decided to try a sneak attack before beginning my change back to human. This again, take a few minutes and I take an additional couple of minutes to get dressed so should someone drive by, there's not this crazy naked woman standing by the side of the road with what most would presume is her poor beat up and abused dog. We werewolves still aren't quite out in the world yet to most folks. They see us as more like the Myrna zombies, something that might or might not exist depending on which particular current conspiracy theory you subscribe to.

Unlocking the car, and fully dressed I get out some water and dried hunks of beef. I have no idea how long she's been running from those bastards but using my push of power always leaves me edgy and needing protein so I figure she needs some too. Last thing I need is an out of control wolf who has gone wild.

It doesn't look like she is volunteering to shift back to human even after eating a large portion of the meat. My cell phone only has about five numbers in it. One is my husband another is Mark. I call Mark and give him a rundown of what's gone on. He agrees with me that these are most likely rogue loners who have formed their own pack for safety and their brand of fun.

"I will be bringing this youngster to you as soon as I can." I tell him. He agrees she needs safety and protection. A submissive wolf will always bring out the dominance in stronger ones, sometimes for the better in protective wolves and sometimes for the worse is less than honorable ones. Submissives can cause dissension and tension in a pack without a strong leader or one with a less than honorable and decent alpha. Mark is as decent as they come even if he isn't the most dominant of alpha's. The little red gold wolf sits at my feet as if she were any other good pet. It's rather disconcerting.

"She's no bigger than a German Shepherd" I tell Mark. She wags her tail at me and grins lifting her lips in a completely non threatening smile. Some people think dogs can't smile. Clearly those folks had never seen a Chesapeake Bay Retriever or Doberman smile before. Mark tells me how I could force her to change, to shift back to human so we can talk but that seems like an assault to me. An invasion of privacy. I won't do it. I tell him I'll see him soon and hang up. She has shrunk down a bit at the last part of the conversation about forcing her to change.

Frowning at her."Don't worry, I won't do that. But know if you won't change back, Mark will force it. I'm sure if only to know who you are and you're story" I follow up with a call to my husband Liam, letting him know the situation. He's a bit miffed at me for as he calls it getting into a fight, but not being a wolf, he doesn't understand there is no way in heaven or earth I could have not intervened. Really he knows that at heart, he just worries for me.

"Well, let's get going it's not getting any cooler out here". I pop the back hatch and she easily hops in. Starting up the air with the engine, we head off down the road. Who knew I would pick up a stray pup today.

Chapter 15
Morning After The Bad Night

"**M**om, do you know Isaac has nightmare's?" Patrick, my oldest son, asks me at breakfast. Issac is the younger of the two teenage werewolves Mark and Cindy have decided to take in and raise as well as train. Liam and I had gone and essentially brought them into the pack's security from being homeless. And with them came a whole new shoe of trouble. Kids with no parents, undocumented, werewolves and a claim of their parents double homicide, along with a human smuggling train.

Without looking at him I respond carefully, hoping to draw more of this new information out "I did not. Has he shared this with you?"

"He mentioned it more in passing. I don't think he meant to." Patrick shrugs. "I think he is afraid of someone in the pack, but that's just more a feeling I get when we are talking about them officially joining."

I keep cooking the eggs I've been working on, mulling it thru. I drop a large chunk of the hard scrambled eggs into a bowl on the floor and crack the next dozen. Bethy creeps up to quickly gobble the offering.

I know a pack run is coming up soon with the full moon. Maybe I should participate this time and try to figure out what's going on.

I too was uneasy at the last formal pack meeting where I spread the word about the A-mpd drugs these zombies are being given. What am I thinking? I do not need to be getting involved in this, they aren't my kids or my problem.

Inwardly I sigh and know I will. It's my way. Somehow I still feel responsible for them.

Isaacs Nightmare

I wake up in a cold sweat, fear dripping off of me as much as water. My brother Ramon stirs in the bed beside me growling slightly from his still human throat. I close my eyes trying to calm my nerves, knowing this nightmare is only behind my eyes, not in front of them. From the night Ramon and I were turned and my parents died. Even though I am fifteen now, I crawl into Ramon's bed to take comfort from his steady presence. Ramon knows I still have nightmares.

We haven't told anyone, even though we are safe now, living with Mark and Cindy. Having been turned in such a brutal fashion while having to watch our parents being torn apart by the werewolf who changed us, has left me with many insecurities and trauma. Every time I change I have a panic attack that still leaves my wolf in control and fearfully aggressive. Only Ramon can really bring my human head back to being in charge over the fear in my animal heart. The nightmare's come less often, but are still very clear and bring with them full movie effects like some super four-D flick The visions include all the scents and sounds of my parents death at the hand of the small wolf who the band of abhorrent men called Thomas.

In my worst dreams I can still hear Thomas' voice in my head saying "Don't worry, I saved your mom for last," followed by laughter. Did he know I had heard him? Did he know he left Ramon and I alive? Did he care?

The dream had subsided for a while, but last month at the pack meeting, which was about us and to determine our fate I guess you could say, there was a scent there. One that I somehow associated with the whole event. It brought it rushing back to the forefront of my memory. I had to leave the room or I was going to be sick. It wasn't quite panic I don't think but darn close.

The dream is always the same. The events replay like some sick twisted memory I can't control. The small wolf has cantered right into the firelight's circle our parents had started, with no fear or hesitation. It looked no different than any other Mexican Lobo even though I had never seen one in person before. Something told me this was different. No wild animal should behave this way. But mom and dad were too tired and too scared at the time to care. Hours ago, we had all just escaped from a human trafficker who had promised to bring us, along with over twenty other people, over the border.

The coyote who was to transport us, was a younger good look-ing man, maybe in his thirties who was well dressed and had made many promises. He had loaded our group into a rental moving van promising all of us freedom on the other side of the border, but instead slamming and chain locking the rolling door. My mom and dad knew we were in trouble then. The promise had been short lived because when the van stopped, we had arrived at some unknown destination rather than the free country he had promised. The man had been joined by others; rougher, dirtier men who carried guns. They began the sorting and trading of the men of our group, yanking men out one by one. There was talk of a labor camp hidden along the Arizona Mexico border.

The younger children were then grabbed and bodily thrown into a smaller van and there was laughter from these captors about the money they would get for this group. There were a couple of grandmothers, abuelas, older women...well lets just say it was worse for them.

Ramon and I, along with our parents had been in the back of the vehicle against the wall, watching as everyone was sorted and separated. Women were crying and begging, children were literally torn away from their parents and the two oldest elderly men had been shot and killed, their only value to serve as a warning to the rest of the group to behave. But my father was smart. He gathered our family into the mix and while the others seemed to be distracted with their sorting and jibes at one another while handling of their human merchandise, my dad, Juan had ushered our small family with a nonverbal hand gesture under the trucks wheels and out the front to run carefully and quietly into the desert. We didn't think anyone had seen us. There was no outcry, no gunfire and no one seemed to be following.

Into the desert we ran, not knowing where we were or how to get to civilization and help. We had taken nothing with us.

Night fell and we were more tired and thirsty than scared at this point. My father, he managed to make a small fire to cook a couple of unwary creatures we had run across in our flight through the desert. The worst part was the not knowing where they were or how far away from any help or civilization we might be. Even border patrol would have been welcome at this point. My father stopped us when it got too dangerous to travel in the absolute blackness that is a desert night without the light pollution a city lends. My poor mother fell asleep quickly in the firelight. Juan, my dad, just sat hunched over staring into the flames while we boys, who had finished our meager meal were beginning to nod off as well. It was then that the small lobo cantered into our camp as if he owned the place. Our dad died quickly and without any screaming or fan fare. One minute he was sitting beside the fire the next the wolf had launched himself on top of him and closed his jaws through his unprotected neck. The look on my father's face was one of surprise rather than fear or pain. I don't think I will ever forget that look. I promised myself I will never forget that look.

Funny, I hadn't remembered that part of the memory until Ellan had come and mind talked to us when she and Liam had first found us.

We had smelled other werewolves in the downtown Phoenix area prior to Ellan and Liam locating us, but we had never seen them. At first we had been afraid of Thomas coming back, finding us, and finish killing us. But the scent of the other wolves we eventually sussed out was different somehow, unique. It still concerned us enough however, that when we would detect one we'd always pick up and move on; or hide since we didn't know about pack or the soon to be familiar wolf musk and canine scents. It was easy to move. Being homeless meant most times people didn't look us in the eye or pay us the slightest bit of attention. We had acquired large backpacks from a homeless agency. We kept our donated clothing and belongings in them, so moving simply meant we picked up and walked to a different homeless encampment in the area for a while until our fears and nervous energy settled down.

Chapter 16
Dinner

A few nights later after Patrick's revelation, Liam and I have invited Mark and Cindy as well as Issac and Ramon over for dinner. Being the last night before the pack hunt the boys are a bit restless as is Mark. Poor Cindy, just as sweet as ever tries to play the peacemaker but as is typical in a teenager household, my boys are stirring the pot. There is rough housing, lots of loud whooping and shouting. Challenges ensue about who can kill the most evil villains and get to the highest level in the current version of Monster Mob 3, some first person killing game. I don't understand it all, but that's okay because according to my boys, I'm old. I just roll my eyes a lot.

Pizzas were ordered delivery for the teenage mini horde. I don't really think four teenagers constitutes a true horde. But what do I know.

The adults enjoy a more civilized meal of steaks with a fresh salad and some corn. Nothing fancy or pretentious. Mark broaches the question first "This is a lovely meal, but would you like to tell me why we are here?" pausing for effect. "In the over 15 years I've known the two of you, we have never shared a meal here in your home." Stabbing a large piece of nearly raw beef. Liam looks to me allowing me to lead the conversation.

"True. But until rather recently our boys weren't werewolves either." A stillness ensued that only a predator hunting prey can effect.

Jack injects quietly from the other room saying "Mom" in an almost warning tone of voice.

"To get right to the point, are you aware Isaac is having nightmares about his and Ramon's being turned? And that those have manifested into a fear based around the pack?"I ask. Cindy continues eating but more slowly and with a guarded look on her face. Mark frowns at me putting his fork down.

"Just how much pack business do you want to be involved in? I thought you didn't want to be pack or Alpha?"

His frown now extending to his forehead, his shoulders tensing. Liam looks between the two of us. Tensions have risen and Mark is ostensibly putting his hackles up. I know he is out of his territory and in mine, where I am the more dominant bitch. Trying for calm "Not at all. And please this is not meant as a slur on you. But I believe that someone in the pack is involved in the trafficking of these people. My other concern is that there were two wolves during our little A-mpd discussion that were actively avoiding any pack contact and left immediately after you did, before Jim could officially close the meeting."Cindy and Mark exchange a quick glance.

Her salad finished, Cindy puts her fork down. Taking a deep breath "Look, I'm no wolf so I can say things others can't." Marks starts to say something but is quickly cut off "No, it's okay Mark, let me get this out. We all need to be on the same page here" The four boys with their werewolf senses have quieted down from the other room. "We know there's something wrong in the pack. And yes it involves two of its members. We are pretty sure it's Ron and Jean but we can't be sure. They don't hunt but they have big fat bank accounts. I get a statement every month from the Crow's Nest on kill numbers and our ten percent coming into the pack. They haven't had a reported kill in over a year, attend only the mandatory meetings but live shall we say very well. I've done some snooping through my contacts in the IRS and again, let me just say something is rotten in Denmark". By the end of her information her nerves have gotten the better of her and she is shaking. Even being aware there is no threat to her, we can all read the shadow of the wolf behind Mark's eyes. His wolf looking to protect his mate from something he has no control over. The boys have all moved to the open entryway no longer pretending to ignore the conversation. Everyone is quiet a moment taking this new information in.

Looking down at my plate and spearing another chunk of steak I say softly "I'd like to be a guest at the next hunt. I'd like Isaac to run with me. I swear to protect him. I want him to point out the specific animals that cause him concern. He's never seen any of the pack so far in their wolf forms, other than Bethy so he will only have scent memory to go off of. No bias. From there we can confirm or deny if your two financially questionable wolves are also involved in Isaac's memories as well." Sticking the piece of speared beef in my mouth I cease talking. Cindy's scent is one of fear but she is no longer quaking and remains steady, looking to her husband to see if this is a good idea.

Isaac puffs up his chest a bit but it's Ramon who steps forward "I can protect my brother just fine." Putting a hand on his brothers arm Isaac looks into his face "You can hermano, but she" he nods at Ellan. "can do it better. Please" He implores his brother.

Jack speaks up "deja que mi mamá haga esto....let my mom do this. You can stay here with us. Papa, Patrick you and I will go on our own hunt further south, out towards the lakes and sands of Yuma" I can feel a tiny push of power from Jack as he makes his impassioned plea. It would seem my children are already forming a sort of pack structure. Only a few months running as wolf and Jack is easily able to push power and not have it flow out of control. My wolf's senses perk up but I can't pursue that now. Right now I have to get Mark to agree to let me do this. For him, for his pack, for Isaac and to find the canker and cut it out.

The room ratchets down a bit as Mark takes a bite of his steak. Chewing thoroughly and swallowing he looks me in the eye saying "Fine, you may hunt with us tomorrow night as my guest."The rest of dinner manages to pass uneventfully. The noise from the boys returns to a jovial ebb and flow as bad guys die, our valiant players get wounded and somehow they all stay friends.

Chapter 17
The Packs Hunt pt 1

The night of the pack hunt is a full moon. I roll my eyes, I can't help it, it is so cliche. It's like can we possibly choose a less here look at me I'm a werewolf night please? But it's Marks pack.

I'm already changed. I told Liam what I planned to do and while he didn't think it was the best of ideas, he acknowledged he didn't have a better option to offer and so he wouldn't stop me. He also had agreed to take our boys and Ramon out in the opposite direction of the Phoenix packs hunt tonight as suggested during last nights dinner.

I walk into the midst of the pack while they are still stripping down and shifting. This is always a dangerous time as wolves feel most vulnerable then. Neither man nor beast, can't flee and really haven't the coordination or ability to fight while in the change. It's a psychological tactic meant to produce anxiety and tension in the wolves who would be concerned with my dominance but the lesser wolves such a Bethy, Kathy or Brian more confident and calmer with their wolves feeling more protected.

I walk into the middle of the packs en mass change, already in full wolf. Isaac is off to one side. His change still takes longer than most being younger, newer and less sure of himself. Without Ramon there tonight I imagine it would have taken longer still. A stalled change can really suck with broken bones, torn skin and fluids leaking. I pad over to where he is, paying no attention to anyone else and lay down. This places myself between him and the rest of the pack. The move puts the rest of the wolves at ease. I don't really expect there to be trouble at this stage but you can't be too careful. Mark as alpha is very trust worthy, and is trusted to keep his pack members safe. That's part of the hallmark of a good leader. Only a few short hours ago he sprang on them the fact I would be joining their monthly hunt as his guest. Simply saying that all wolves needed the company of a pack. It's as good a cover as any. And not untrue. I just hate mass pack hunts after my experience with the Los Angles' so called pack.

Bethy and Kathy have both completed their changes in their vehicles quickly and come up to me touching noses and wagging tales. I return the greeting with quick licks to their muzzles and fur ruffling whiffles. Kathy's husband and mate Greg is a huge wolf easily three hundred pounds. He towers over my wolf in form, which to be fair is also on the larger size. It's odd but I've never known a wolf to be so clumsy. His harsh gray and black coat is rather nondescript. Kathy on the other hand is almost a shining radiant blond. Her color of creams, whites and what could only be described as cinnamon coalesces into this stunning color combination topped off with solid black whiskers and nose tip. She is one of Mark's "on camera" wolves.

Being smaller and just as stunning is Bethy only in a different way. Mark has used these two ladies as public relations wolves. The ones the news outlets have professional stills of. Kathy has even done public demonstrations and gone with Mark to some of the political meetings to help smooth things out, to put a friendly face on the werewolf. I just roll my eyes a lot. Let's face it, if most of the public knew we could be a three hundred pound clumsy, likely to break you out of sheer dumb luck as aggression monster, things might have gone very differently for us. Greg is still changing and Kathy returns to take up a place by her mate.

William finishes his change a bit earlier than some of the other males and advances toward me. He has always been leery of me in either form. I hop to my feet not quite allowing myself as a guest to display fang. As forth or fifth in the structure, he's not a real threat to me but my job is to protect Isaac through his first official pack hunt while hoping he can identify the scent or scents that have made him so uneasy.

William stops a full wolfs body length away. I don't remember if he has a mate in the pack or not but he is a welder by trade and his wolf is equally well muscled, if not more so, than when he is in his human skin. My guess is he could be higher up in the structure if he choose to be. Williams level tail and body stance indicate curiosity more than aggression. I give a big single tail thump to reassure him and drop my mouth open in an easy light pant. He moves along waiting for the rest of his pack to finish their changes.

Once everyone has completed their change and wriggled and shaken the last of the tingles and aches out, Mark picks up his head scenting the air in anticipation of leading off tonight's hunt. This is his favorite place to hunt and members of the pack can often be found running here so everyone is overall at ease. This area has remarkably been left to nature being on the far side of Lake Pleasant and entering the Hell's Canyon preserve area. Its pristine desert is home to quite a lot of wildlife from wild burros, large lynx, even an odd bear or two at times.

Mark lifts his head giving a deep but short howl, collecting the pack and myself together. We move out as a unit towards a deep arroyo whose walls are easily four feet with a basin of packed gravel. Isaac and I stay to the outside of the main grouping but I think to find the wolf who is the cause of Isaac's instinct's to become alert, even fearful we will have to mingle. I move towards the middle of the group bringing Isaacs wolf with me. He is a smaller gray-gold wolf that has a single white back paw.

We glide into the pack seamlessly along the outer edges. Lesser wolves giving way to my more dominant presence, while the more dominant wolves continue to stay at the front of the pack just behind Mark. Greg tripping a few times from the fast pace Mark is keeping. Isaac finally eases into an almost galloping gait to keep up, that we are using to eat the miles quickly.

Soon we run across a fresh trail from a rather large band of javelina and all the wolves perk up, knowing a hunt is on. Killing the wild javelina helps keep their populations in check and damage of the surrounding areas to a minimum. When the housing and water laws changed and forced people into more tightly knit areas of the Phoenix basin, these wild boars exploded due to few natural predators being left. Now they are considered pests much in the same way as mice and rats are. My stomach roils.

I have instructed Isaac to indicate when he scents whomever troubles him and to let me know, but so far it seems nothing other than a case of new wolf nerves is bothering our youngster. He has been trailing at my shoulder the whole run and I can feel his excitement picking up along with the rest of the packs. There is a synchronicity to it I can feel but I can't participate in not being an accepted part of the pack. I have no place within their structure so I have to take all my cues from the others body language.

Wolves stalk prey in silence and so within the pack even footfalls seem muffled as the acrid scent of the peccaries tells us we are very close now. Being dark they will be most active and alert and dangerous. Wild peccaries, I think to myself *is there a tame variety?,* have been known to kill joggers and teenagers out for fun. But my past experiences are haunting me and my mind is wandering in memories. Isaac's step stutters and he slows his pace bumping his head into my side bringing me back to the present. I look at him *"What is it?"*

His eyes flit over to Anthony as he ducks his head. A rather large tan and brown wolf running just to the front of us now. Since the pack has slowed down a bit to gain a more cautious approach he is close enough for his individual scent to reach Isaac. Anthony I know. He is a big construction worker, single, with a rather nasty sense of humor, one even bordering on cruel. Anthony is again in that nebulous forth fifth or sixth space within the packs structure. Interesting as both Ron and Jean are hunting with us today and Isaac has basically ignored them. Those were the two Mark had concerns about, not Anthony. I can't take too much time mulling that one over as we have crossed the dry river bed approaching a huge clump of what appears to be recently felled mesquite trees with the band of javelinas we've been tracking doing a brilliant job of rearranging the already softened earth. Even from my point of view, I can make out over a dozen different animals who are not too thrilled to suddenly find their meal time interrupted by a bunch of wolves. Immediately there is teeth clacking and growling to be heard. This close to the band their musky smell is almost overwhelming to the nose. I'm glad Isaac was able to identify at least one of the wolves prior to this fight.

The stinky piggy creatures form a large circle using the felled trees as back protection. Pretty smart for a bunch of pigs. We wolves run on the outside taking slashing leaps at them every now and then. Their fearsome canine teeth are as long as ours and they are mean. Mark did not pick an easy fight. These creatures will defend themselves ferociously. Our pack has over a dozen wolves but so does theirs and they have no human head or heart to take into consideration. For them this is a fight to the death. I'm not sure this was a good plan but we seem to be committed to it now.

Several of the bolder wolves are making feint attacks attempting to draw one of more of the javelinas away from the safety of their band. As soon as one wolf feints in this draws a returning slash and charge from one or more of the prey. Another wolf attempts to hamstring the separated peccary. This goes on for a bit in maddening repetition of feint, draw back, charge and slash. Neither side gaining any real advantage. The lower ranked wolves really have no play in this theater and so maintain an outward perimeter. I stay to the outside of this seeing no point to harassing the pigs.

My mind wanders to the last day I was with the Los Angeles pack, and why I left them.

Chapter 18
The Los Angeles Experience

I had heard of the Los Angeles Pack and I didn't know any other wolves at the time. Part of me longed for others of my kind. I never knew who made me though I now understood and appreciated why. At the time, I had convinced Liam that this was something I needed to do. I hadn't met Mark yet or known a whole lot about what I was or what I could do. At times I would rage almost out of control. I was afraid for my toddler son and husband and I felt I had to find some answers. This wasn't something you searched for on the internet. But years of law enforcement and training also told me to be careful and not lay all my cards on whatever table I found. So I decided on a plan that I hoped would keep my family safe and me as well.

Los Angeles never developed the water plan that Arizona had and so it's population was still scattered and stretched with large swaths of land in between cities and freeways. Driving to Anaheim I rented a hotel for three weeks. I figured that was the absolute longest I would stay away from my family. I chose a middle grade hotel by one of the large theme parks, believing no one would question a tourist staying that length of time. I made sure the hotel had the type of key card system where you simply waved the credit card shaped key over the touch-less pad allowing my wolf the ability to enter the room at will without having to change. Being in wolf form felt safer to me.

When I am in my four footed guise I am stronger and more confident. My human form was older being fifty years of age, less agile and carried the damage of old injuries. My wolf is surprisingly agile and virtually pain free.

What I didn't realize or account for is there is no actual single pack. I found that out the first day. It's more a conglomeration of six or seven loosely formed gangs with all the blood, gore, death and violence you believe that entails. I was very naive about it all.

This was the time the Myrna zombies were still being mostly covered up by the government and we were all told it would be okay. Wolves had really just come out to the public.

That first night I changed and went looking, for what I really didn't know. My wolf slunk down streets and alleyways following scents here and there until several hours later, I came upon a trio of wolves out hunting. At first as I approached they bristled and snarled, but curiosity got the better of them and they encircled me sniffing and sizing me up. I am a large wolf of dusty brown and tans, nothing special but my size I think intimidated them. Maybe not, maybe I am giving myself too much credit. However after a while one with a gray muzzle and black feet brushed up against me giving me the body language I understood to be follow them. I ran with this group of wolves for the entire time, twice returning to my hotel, retrieving my key from under the bumper of my car where I had hidden it to gain entry. I would call Liam checking in with him and video facing with the baby. Reassuring him all was well, but I think he knew. Think he instinctively felt I was not content nor comfortable where I was. He was in the same former profession I was and had learned to read these same cues like I had.

These wolves, this pack, was huge in my estimation. Over thirty animals in total. And they would harass and torment other wolves who weren't a part of their group. Didn't matter what form they were in, human or wolf. The top three leaders were firmly entrenched but the remainder was very fluid. Dominance fights broke out daily including knife fights, beatings and even the disappearance of one wolf that no one seemed to question.

Being the latest acquisition, as I learned I was; I kept my head down, my body posture as neutral as I knew how. I joined in the running but refused to participate in the harassment of others. Several of the middle level wolves tried to harass me to take part but I staunchly refused, though to my shame neither did I interfere or stop it. The most dominant ones left me alone, as if they couldn't be bothered with the weaker most submissive wolves. We were beneath their notice. However we were fair game from the middle and lower end wolves who found encouragement among their peers.

Most nights consisted of running in wolf form along the many piers and beaches. Los Angeles had imposed a curfew from midnight to four for some reason years ago and just never lifted it, so there wasn't as much of a chance of running into humans as you might think. Other single wolves were fair game for harassment and any Myrna found was torn down by a joint pack effort. Now that, I actively engaged in and learned quickly how dangerous these things really were.

One bite and a wolf was doomed. It made rabies look like a mild case of the sniffles. A wolf in full rage would kill anything in its path and had to be destroyed. One such occurrence it took the pack many hours to not only kill the now enraged wolf but the other's he had infected along the way as well. There was a swath of death and destruction all from a pack member getting grabbed and a single bite to the nose from a Myrna zombie.

On the nights the pack was bored and not finding things to kill or chase they made their own games. Something I despised, was their habit of stalking and attacking sleeping groups of seals. They would sneak up on a group of sleeping seals, almost always four to six animals, cutting them off from their escape into the ocean. The cold ocean was always their first choice of escape from us.

The seals with their thick skins and layer of blubber made the wolves work to score deep blood rending gashes but that never deterred the pack. Terrorizing these poor creatures was pointless and often at least one of them died from their wounds. During these assaults I would hang back and keep my distance not joining the fray. Anyone who heard or saw the attacks would quickly turn away for fear of being next. If a seal couldn't defend itself how could a human. It was like watching a sharks feeding frenzy only on land. They struck the large awkward animals again and again drawing excitement and satisfaction at their panicked and piteous cries. For some reason these large animals never seem to fight back, not that they'd have any real chance being on land and so outnumbered. Finally a large male has worked himself close enough to the edge of the pier and with a herculean twist of his body grabs the nearest wolf dragging it into the ocean with him. The remaining seals take advantage of the momentary distraction and fling themselves into the water as well, disappearing beneath the dark and now murky depths. One particularly prey driven determined wolf almost follows them but stops with his toes on the very edge of the pier balancing precariously. I thought to myself *we really are monsters.*

The leaders trotted back down the pier, across the sand to a grassy area reserved for picnickers during the daytime hours. Everyone followed and flopped down in some weird imitation of ....broken marionettes.

It was then that a larger wolf, easily over two hundred pounds approached me. I ignored him keeping my head down and body still. I haven't' yet really had to fight for my position and I am not sure how my wolf body will react to my commands.

He moves as if to walk by me, but instead at the last moment leaping over me landing on top of me grabbing the back of my neck. My eyes flare with surprise, then power. I rise up at the same time my mind screams *"oh hell no you bitch!"* The offending wolf is thrown off tearing a small portion of my neck ruff out. Before he can safely land on his feet, I am on him biting every single bit I can, over and over again while a wave of power spreads through me outward to the rest of the wolves all of whom turn their heads from me and drop to their bellies. The large gray wolf is now freely bleeding from multiple lacerations to his face and head. His left ear is hanging on only by the exposed cartilage. Blood runs more than drips and he lays down exposing his throat to me while he makes deep whines of supplication. *"I should kill you where you lay you piece of filth".* My energy is radiating so strongly that not a single wolf has moved. I let my frustration and fear and rage seep over me biting him one more time through his muzzle crushing it at the nose tip, knowing it may well be a fatal wound. All he can do is scream in pain and fear rooted to the spot through my will alone. I stand up fully and look over the rest of the pack still immobilized, and snarl. I was a fool to think the Los Angeles packs had anything I needed. I was done with this sham. Turning I walked slowly stiff legged from the group of frozen wolves. The entire pack motionless due to my push of dominance, power and rage.

Back at my hotel, grabbing my key card from under my rental cars bumper, I wave it in front of the pad. Using my paw to push down on the handle and open the door I let myself in and begin my change. I grit my teeth through the pain to shift back into humanity. I need my husband and child to remind me why we don't kill things, even those preternatural creatures who might deserve it.

It is time to go home.

Chapter 19
The Packs Hunt pt 2

My mind returns to present day when at some unseen cue, Mark raises his head giving a couple of sharp yips more akin to what a coyote might do and bounds off as fast as he can. The rest of the pack follows in sure pursuit with the band of seriously annoyed peccaries hot on all our tails.

Mated pair Greg and Kathy bring up the rear as the slowest wolves, who are in danger of falling under a pair of razor like tusks. Unseen by me, Mark has circled back and makes a dangerous and stupid diversion to dash between the last pack member and the rapidly advancing matriarch of the peccaries distracting her in into following him for a short distance, giving the slower pair a chance to get safely away.

The pack races up the side of the arroyo we've been following and we find ourselves in another little ghost town abandoned for water rights. Buildings decaying, left to molder with even a few decrepit skeletonized cars. Nerves are still high from what was essentially a harry and dash from the javelinas and some of the wolves are tense and still ready to fight. I drop back to an outside edge, bringing Isaac with me so we don't run afoul of any stray tempers that might flair.

Having run once for a few weeks in the Los Angeles pack, they would not have backed off until every single animal in the peccary band was dead and eaten (*ick)* and even then there still would have been a few nasty blood letting fights between the pack members. It's all very post apocalyptic. The strong survive, the weak die macho crap over there, and I couldn't stay because eventually almost every wolf there would have challenged me and I would have had to kill them, taking control of the pack. Not in my game plan. I hope Mark has planned a way to work off the packs combined excitement and prey drive. We had all parked our cars at the far edge of Lake Pleasant and now we were deep into Hell's Canyon Wilderness, miles from any real cities or towns. We hadn't to my knowledge, even passed any overnight campers, which was good, never a fun time explaining twenty or so wolves running through your camp. And yet somehow it always, without fail, gets caught on video. It's almost a badge of honor to find your wolf self on some internet site running through some poor slobs camp site or back yard. I'm sure there is a betting pool somewhere.

Slowing the pace to more of a wander, gives everyone time to sniff around, meander a bit and just enjoy the closeness of the pack. A frightened jackrabbit bolts ahead of a small group of the wolves and they bound after it. A few birds take flight as others sniff and snuffle in the bushes. We hear a coyote pack yip several times in warning but they stay far clear of us. Isaac finds a burrow that's part of a much larger prairie dogs network of dens. He begins digging and several prairie dogs come out a few feet away chattering and squeaking warnings to their den mates. From there, basically it turns into a large game of whack the prairie dog with the wolves losing their deadly intensity and dangerous edge to becoming happier and more content.

Isaac seems to have grown bored with his prairie dog hole and moved on to leaping at an overhanging branch of a lone pine tree. The kid has too much energy for me. I lay down with my head on my paws and doze a bit.

Growing bored as well and with the impending dawn, Mark indicates its time to head back to the cars. His pace is one of an easy lope that no one has any problems keeping up with even this far into the early morning.

Isaac and I hang back once we are at the cars, allowing the others to change. Once changed most dress quickly while eating hunks of their favorite jerky or whatever they have brought with them. Some give handshakes to Mark and drive off, others form small groups talking about the javelinas. Finally just Mark, Jim the packs second and Joseph the packs third remain. I begin my change and indicate Isaac to do so as well. Once back on two feet as opposed to four we all gather around Marks cooler tearing up large chunks of meat and cheese.

A few minutes of feeding refuel our hungry bodies, and I open the conversation we all know has to happen. "It's Anthony." I say.

Brows furrow. Looks are exchanged. "Are you sure?" Joseph asks. Joseph is what I consider to be third in the packs structure and a guy I have liked ever since meeting him. He's young-ish, which to me means he is just hitting thirty. He's been a wolf for as long as I've known him, which is just around ten years so I am guessing he choose to be changed like my boys did at the age of consent, rather than facing forced citizenship service and mandatory antiserum injections.

Joseph looks at Mark who is clearly searching his memory for any-thing, any clue that Anthony could be involved in illegal trafficking. Isaac just stands there eating his pizza not looking at anyone. That's the nice thing about an all meat pizza, it doesn't need to be reheated. Someday I think his wolf will be dominant enough to challenge Joseph but at fifteen he is still feeling his way around and stands by me for the support he needs. Especially as we are basically accusing one of Marks pack of illegally trafficking humans into the country!

Shaking his head Mark looks at us "I'd like to do some digging before we go accusing anyone, NOT that I am saying you are wrong hijo" he interjects, when Isaac stops eating at his words and looks up at him. He commences chewing with a new look of defiance on his face.

Tired, I reply "I've had my fill of this for the day thank you. What on earth were you thinking by attacking a javelina pack? For crying out loud, they didn't bother us." again recalling my brief time in the Los Angeles pack, Marks seeming random attack on the wild pigs had unnerved me more than a little, though it ended well enough.

"It's a great strengthening exercise." He responds, trying to let the accusation he hears roll off him. Jim bristles a bit at the implied allegation but takes his cue from Mark. "We didn't actually hurt them. They were only scared a little, now they'll be more wary of us, and my wolves got a great work out and practice in working together." Finishing his explanation he stares at me in a way he wouldn't normally do. He is a little more upset about his leadership being challenged than he'd like to admit. Joseph and Isaac stop chewing, both keeping their heads down. Jim takes a step back giving room for a fight to occur.

A few seconds extends longer than might be good for either of us, but I blink and turn my head away "Fine, good, yeah, sorry. Not my place to question how you run your pack. It just reminded me of something unpleasant".

Gently "Your time in LA?" he asks. Joseph and Isaac look at each other having not heard this story but are unable to ask. I give a little shiver, mentally straiten up and continue the original conversation. "Okay, so Anthony. You do what you need to do to find out what's there. Do the boys need to come over to our place for a while?"

Isaac's face lights up at this, my boys and Ramon and Isaac have struck up a friendship over online gaming and table top role playing games that has made them fairly inseparable at times. Mark smiles but replies "Sorry kiddo, no can do. She lives too far away from your school." His face falls a little bit.

Chapter 20
The Call Of Blood

A week has gone by since the pack hunt. Mark has called this morning. Another body has been found. This time it's just east of Sierra Vista in the San Pedro Riparian National Conservation area. More than just mauled, torn apart and stinking of fear and pain. A few of these bodies had been attributed by the humans to the small bear population or large wild cats of the area. But this time, for the last several weeks, Mark and the Durango Packs Alpha have been working together looking specifically for the scent markers of the former pack mate Anthony.

Anthony had suddenly disappeared after Isaac had identified him as being a part of the human smuggling chain that had lead to the killing of his parents and the turning of his brother Ramon and himself into werewolves. I didn't ask what happened to Anthony, nor did I really care. Involved in human trafficking, murder and worse didn't really rank high on my sympathy scale. All that mattered was we find this leader, this Alpha wolf who was conducting this like some sick psychopathic orchestra for his personal pleasure.

Mark had told Ellan and I that Anthony was a multipurpose fellow who would drive, hold captive, help sort as well as distribute their human cattle. Those that got out of line, this Thomas, this alpha would kill to make an example of but that he, nor anyone he knew, had ever seen him in his human skin. Only wolf. We didn't have much to go on, only a general location but when a couple more bodies had shown up we knew we were on the right trail.

Thomas' Beginning

Men Women Children It didn't matter. He enjoyed them all. The panic, the pain, the fear. The feel of flesh rending between his teeth like nothing more than poorly woven cloth.

He had always enjoyed killing things. Cats, dogs even goats and pigs. They all made such delightful sounds and gyrations when he was torturing them.

But it wasn't until he had become a werewolf that he truly learned the joy of the kill. That first kill had shown him how very powerful he was. People had always feared him even as a child. Avoided him, whispered about him, their lizard hind brain knew he was a predator and they were nothing to him but prey.

Growing up middle class he had lacked for nothing. Neither food, nor clothing, toys, schooling or even loving stable parents. But neither was he truly accepted in anyone's eyes but his own. When the werewolf had found him, he was busy torturing another of the neighborhood's poor dogs. This one a big shepherd mix who had ceased fighting back a long time ago and could only ki'yi in terror and pain at each new stroke of the blade.

The werewolf had broken onto the scene and given Thomas a taste of what he had been doing to that poor creature. In retrospect Thomas was sure the werewolf thought him dead when it had left him and released the hound to return to its loving home. But alas, he did not die. And so into the world was born a truly terrible killer. His change took longer than normal. Guess the other wolf believed he had done the job. Leaving Thomas in a bloody mess in the back alleyway. But once reformed into the four footed creature of stealth and power; a new killing machine had been born. After the first initial change Thomas was dumbfounded. He could hear so much more, see so much more even if colors were a bit muted. But what he could smell, now that was life changing. The blood, such a scent as he had never imagined. It carried all kinds of wonderful new information to his wolf's brain and senses. The fear and pain exploded into his mind from not just the droplets but the entire world was saturated in this new and wonderful scent. His nose also now telling him things he never knew existed.

Another new thing, was the scent of the werewolf who had changed him. His brain "knew" what this was. He trailed this other scent all the way to his home street. And there, just three doors down. There, washing his car, in human form was the werewolf who had given him this wonderful gift. Trotting up to him, not sure how to communicate in this new form he stared at the other. But rather than finding a welcome from a fellow killer, he saw only revulsion at the knowledge of what had been done. Shame and fear, then anger. These things Thomas knew about but could read more acutely in this, his new body. The wolf in human guise started to back up dropping the hose, looking for either a weapon or an escape. Neither of which Thomas would permit.

Thomas knocked the man down between the car and garage, making for a reasonable shield between them and the rest of the world and then proceeded to tear into the soft flesh with tooth and claw in a joyous fashion at doing the bloody deed himself. The new found scents of fear and pain stimulated the attack further until well after the body had stopped moving. The blood flowing readily to mix with the still running hose to wash down the drive to the gutter. This was his first human kill. And he relished the thought of his next. Feeling his own self worth and importance. He ambled a while before turning towards home, his tail moving quickly side to side already anticipating his next two kills.

Chapter 21
Tracking Prey

I was the better tracker. Ellan is much more of a point and shoot kind of gal.

It made more sense to track down this evil creature and kill him as quickly as possible. Before he could do more harm. Anthony, the wolf who was finally made to reveal his dark secrets presumably to Mark and Jim prior to his mysterious or not so dissappearance, had said this Thomas was pure evil with no remorse or care. That only the power that came from human trafficking and the selling of the zombie drug A-mpd was what gave him any pleasure. He would kill a woman or child as easily and with less thought than it took to kill a fly. Well, two could play that game. Ellan and I were completely on the same page. There was no bringing this wolf into the Crow's Nest for arrest and prosecution. There was no bringing in local law enforcement. Ellan and I had agreed this man had to die. Being outside of a packs formal structure gave us a large advantage while not putting a target on Mark's back, nor making him responsible should something go wrong somehow. With both our boys now turned wolf, we felt calmer about going out to hunt like this. Our boys were safe.

Tracking this bastard has been more time consuming and difficult than we had originally thought. My wolf needed some rest and protein. I was never too healthy. Being wolf helped but I was still subject to the same infirmities. We had started at the remains of the most recent known kill. Scent was all over it and not just the poor boys. It had taken us around six hours of active tracking to get to this point. The problem being now that we had found the outlaw rogue's trail it was very hard not to rush in looking for the kill. We have the advantage it seems.

Thomas was finishing his newest and latest kill, playing in it really. There was hardly enough left of the body to be able to call it once human. And by all the pretty red splatters this too had been a young teen. Could easily have been our young Isaac just months before. Just a child. Not even a Myrna, which would have justified the kill. But then we knew this wolf by reputation, and that reputation was pure evil. No one we knew had ever seen this wolf in his human guise but his scent was now known to us. He didn't try to hide it from his kills, and those were numerous. Wild and unique, strong and musky this wolf was obviously a dominant who could have been an alpha in his own right. Whether he was just sadistic and a natural born serial killer, or something had happened over time no one knew. He didn't hold a traditional pack, only a loose group of rag tag disgruntled toughs. The classic jack booted thugs if you will. Some wolves, some not.

He was not much larger than a traditional Mexican wolf, maybe weighing in at one hundred pounds, confirming Isaac's memory to be accurate. His coat is black on top graying out on the sides down to a brush colored dun on his underside, neck and legs. My thought is this is how he gets so close to people, they see nothing but a regular wolf and stop to take pictures or even feed it, not realizing exactly what they are offering up as food.

Ellan and I fight together all the time, me typically as wolf, her as human but almost exclusively to kill Myrna's. Hunting one of your own, with the intent to slaughter is a bit different. A wolf who is not entirely stable or lower than the one being fought could by swayed or dominated into submission and easily killed. But we know several beta's and gamma's have gone against Thomas with less than successful results. Thomas was the name he'd been called by, I'm not really sure if it was his real name. Thomas had been killing normal humans on a regular basis, most of those teenagers or younger. Their remains would be torn to bits, chunks of flesh missing, presumed eaten. The poor corpses always stinking of pain, desperation and terror.

Mark had asked us, after having to return the remains of the Durango Mexico's packs second and third, to kill this foul creature. Juan had sent his two highest ranking wolves after Thomas just a week prior and they had tracked him into Arizona. It was when we returned the remains he learned more of the story of this wolf's travels. First thru South America into Mexico up into Texas back thru Mexico which is when Juan got involved and now into Arizona. According to the information, no less than forty bodies have been attributed to this wolf. Since no one's seen him in his human guise it was originally thought he was lost to his wolf, but Mark now knows this is not the case.

Wolves who become lost to their wolf essentially go on a killing spree, much like the Myrna's until they themselves are killed. There is a sickness of their scent, most other wolves can easily distinguish and if they are part of a pack, they are dealt with. Since no one is sure how dominant Thomas is, Mark wasn't comfortable sending his second and third or even himself for fear of loosing control of the Phoenix pack entirely. He still has a problem or two to deal with himself within the pack, but neither can we let this opportunity slip by. The Durango pack had already taken a great risk by sending theirs across borders without Mark's knowledge or consent, and what had been found led him to believe this loner was not lost to his wolf but very deliberately a sadistic fiend. Ellan and I happened to agree with him.

When wolves fight there's a certain amount of ritual sizing up that takes place. A testing of the waters. Who's faster, who's more dominant, more experienced. Fights can often be determined before any actual fang or claw rends flesh on these pre-trial posturings. It's when two wolves who are virtually equal in that dominant role that skills, size, speed, knowledge, treachery and how much leeway the wolf portion of our brains control come more into play. Sadly the human aspect of our nature rarely rules our hearts. Wolf packs are still built on and around this balance. It is important. Everyone needs to know where their place is in the world, in the pack and in general. An unbalanced pack will implode and quickly take out most of its middle wolves in the process. This is one of many reasons there are a limited number of well run packs and so many lone wolves or mated pairs. It takes a strong alpha to truly hold a group of lesser dominant ones together. Zeta wolves are uber submissive and fairly rare, though the Phoenix pack seems to have more than its fair share. Not often welcomed into a pack unless female, zeta's are often seen as prey when found as lone wolves but even in packs they can inadvertently stir up trouble because some feel the need to protect while others want to dominate or even drive off or kill. The wolf aspect of some seeing them as too weak and a liability to the pack. In human form it is easier, as our human heads can use logic and civility to rule our animal hearts.

We take a rest for a moment under a deep sage bush. The space having been recently occupied by a pair of jackrabbits unhappy to have been evicted by us. Ellan gives me the rest of the dried beef she has brought and the water from our supply. We have tracked the intruder to somewhere between Tombstone and Bisbee. Having begun this hunt earlier in the day back in Sierra Vista, it is wearing on me. Six hours is a long time to single-mindedly track a suspect.

It is surprising how desolate it still is in this day and age. The rest of Arizona seems to have been filled in and paved over. But out here is still bare naked desert. Just sand, scrub brush and dirt. We are also only a few miles from the Mexico border out here but thankfully close enough to still get cell reception, as my mate texts Mark to keep him apprised. I briefly wonder which side of the border that poor child was from and who will have to be made to notify his family. They are sure to be waiting and worrying. Just glad it isn't us. Even though performing this task for the Phoenix pack, we have never formally become a park of the pack.

After spotting our prey we keep going for a bit so as to hopefully not alert him to our presence, or at the very least our purpose. Ellan is carrying her weapon of choice, the antique 357 six shooter.

Barely June but Arizona is already giving us one hundred degree temperatures. Problem is, I don't do so well in the heat any more and it shows. I am panting quite a lot and the bare shade of this bush does little to offer me respite. My furry body is hotter than a normal humans and even with a good helping of protein we are still going to need to act soon. Ellan recognizes this as well. Her face a mask of concern. "We need to flank him like we do the Myrna's but I have to have a clear shot. I won't risk hitting ...."

Chapter 22
Our Task, Complete

Before the sentence can finished, my wife is violently pushed to the ground, face down with the black and gray wolf loner we had intentionally passed on top of her. Biting at her hip and belt. He easily severs through the tough leather belt flinging the weapon still in its holster to the ground, behind all of us with a quick flip of his head. He steps back from my mate and sits, allowing his tongue to loll out the side of his mouth, mockery evident in every line of his body language.

I have whirled to face him with a snarl, thinking to distract him so Ellan can retrieve the gun, but apparently she has other plans. I can feel her outrage and indignation. A brief look her way and I can tell from the amassed power fluctuations, she is intending to change. Well Damn, this isn't what we planned. We have no way of knowing how experienced a fighter he is, and clearly he is more experienced at sneaking up on us than either anticipated. I take a step towards Thomas wanting to draw his attention while leaning away from my mate. He isn't taking the bait.

It's like he is waiting for her to change, his intent and focus on her. I am less than 3 feet from him. Gathering myself together I take the opportunity to strike at him, snarling and snapping at anything he lets me get close to. Evidently my rash rush annoys him. He lowers his head while getting to his feet, pinning his ears back. Yellow eyes now focused on me. His movements are deliberate and intense as he stalks closer to me looking for an opening. I dance in, snapping at a leg and rush back out again before he can get a hold of me. Each rush, I give a little ground he gains a little, but the dance step is giving my mate the needed minute of time to shift form.

A couple of minutes in a fight is a really long time. In my head I hear laughter but it's not coming from my mate. I freeze startled, no one has ever spoken or communicated like my mate does. In that moments hesitation, Thomas succeeds in grabbing my shoulder. With one back and forth slash, he tears a large deep gash in it. A flap falls open revealing the muscle and fat beneath. It bleeds freely, the rich scent of my blood momentarily overwhelming my senses. In that space of time he was distracted with his attack on me, my mate is suddenly on top of Thomas. Her weight drives his smaller frame to the ground. Sheer hate and malice in her eyes, her mouth fully around Thomas' muzzle including covering his eyes. Her larger frame and jolting hold on his head, neck and shoulders throwing off his balance, causes his snout to dig into the ground. He is forced to readjust his stance just to remain upright. The wild flare of anger that had allowed my mate to change has settled on her like a cloak of power. I am not immune even though all of her rage and dominance is centered on the wolf she's currently grinding into the dirt. I back off, to lessen the effects of that rage as her order sounds clearly in my brain *"Submit"*. Normal prey when their face and nose is compromised back up and thrash their heads. This one clearly fought with his human intelligence and tried to roll my mate off of him more like a crocodile, but her sheer size and determined hold prevented him from completing the maneuver.

Thomas tries to get up but Ellan has her hold on him and refuses to loosen or be shaken off. Blood starts flowing more freely from the puncture wounds on his muzzle and through one of his eyes as she grinds her jaws more tightly shut. Now wildly thrashing his head back and forth he tries backing up. The smaller wolf is desperate to dislodge her hold, panic beginning in the edges of his mind. Her order rang thru his brain but he hasn't lived this long, like this, to give in without a fight. And fight he did. Whipping his head wildly back and forth in an attempt to get her off, he responds in kind. *"Never"*.

I can hear his response, feel the indignation and the hate roll off of him. I've never known another wolf with enough power to be able to speak like this. I have never seen a wolf fight her compulsion this way. Never known a wolf with the strength of will and dominance to mind talk the way Ellan can. It's no wonder so many dominant wolves have fallen to him. I can understand how other's failed to bring him in or kill him. But Ellan is not a force to be ignored. He tries to flip my mate off. He attempts to roll but Ellans large size means she can easily stand over him, control him, while keeping her hold on his muzzle, her eye teeth puncturing the bones and flesh crushing him slowly.

Thomas's nasal airway is being restricted; crushed and his breathing is getting heavier. He is forced to open his mouth to pant to get any air. His entire muzzle is dragging further in the dirt making a trench in the light sandy soil. He is completely blind as well. My mate now shakes her head back and forth in great sweeping strokes as if wiping the ground with his muzzle using her weight and control to further throw Thomas off balance, ensuring he is unable to lift his head effectively. His once wild thrashing becoming more a desperate scuttle backwards while his legs tremble. Seeing my opportunity I lunge in low, to grab his throat to further impede his airway. His thick neck fur and muscles keep the immediate damage down to a minimum but I hold on, chewing my way inward.

His own thrashing causes as much damage as my chewing. Beset on top and bottom by merciless fang and weight, it is all Thomas can do is stay on his feet, and even that is short lived. As he collapses partially on top of me, I feel his great vein give way beneath my embedded fangs as it begins to spew its vital blood within his own body, torn in half.

Ellans voice in my head and I am sure his as well "*Make no mistake, I was always going to kill you.*"

And die he did with blood pouring out his nose and mouth, once his lifeless remains are released by the both of us. Ellan lets go of his nose more slowly still growling at the audacity of this evil creature to think he could resist her order. The huge puncture wounds in his skull and mangled bone evidence of her intent. I lean over to nuzzle Ellan and get a short growl and snap as a rebuff. Okay the wolf is still ascendant. Time for another tact. I lift the paw of the damaged shoulder and give a short whine and she focuses on the blood still oozing from the fang's slice. It's not deep thankfully, but is long. The flap of skin making it more dynamic in appearance than it is in reality.

Turning around without a sound she trots off into the surrounding desert. Not quite the reaction I was looking for. I am left a bit perplexed, not sure what to do next. I need to find some shade and water soon, and the car is several miles back almost all the way to Sierra Vista. I recognize I don't have enough reserves left to make that trip myself and even shifting back, I'll be stark naked in the Arizona desert, well off the beaten path. This is not shaping up to be a pretty site.

However, in short order Ellan returns with a full grown jackrabbit in her mouth. Dropping it at my feet she take two steps back and dips her head indicating it's for me. She trots off again, once I pick up the rabbit returning to our semi shaded side of the bush and begin eating the fresh meat. Before I am done she returns once more, dropping a big lizard in the place the rabbit formerly lay. I look at it, my human sense a bit unhappy about this choice of meal, but I am feeling better. She nuzzles me quickly once and I hear *"Going for the car, stay"*. I wish I could respond in kind because being told to stay is a bit irksome. I am not a pet poodle after all. But necessary I suppose. I settle in to eat the largish reptile, wondering exactly where she got this from.

I am dozing lightly after the fight and impromptu meal, but protein is protein. The sun seems to be falling a bit lower in the sky as I hear a car approach. I recognize the engine sounds of our van. How on earth Ellan managed to get back to the car, change and drive out here to get me, I don't know but I can sure appreciate. I am still hot and thirsty. The van slows to a stop allowing the side sliding door to open. I hop in, into the blessed air conditioning running at full blast. My mate has a big square metal bowl of water there and several pounds of raw steak. She really knows how to make me feel better. My shoulder wound has closed over but thankfully isn't serious and should mostly heal during my next change. Now to tell Mark and the Mexican pack the good news.

Chapter 23
Weary Returns

S tanding underneath the cascading water I listen to Liam relaying to Mark the days events. I have had to force two changes today and just want to wash the scent of that foul creature off my skin and to sink into oblivion in my own bed now I am home and Liam and I are safe. I think to myself *We are just monsters of a different flavor. We tracked him and we killed him.*

The conversation is long and detailed. The shower eventually runs out of hot water even with our solar tank. It's Arizona, so water is never really cold. But in the interest of water conservation, I turn it off and turn to exit the tiled stall. Liam walks towards me. He slept as the wolf all the way home gathering his strength back, having gorged himself on about five pounds of raw steak. I had walked with him the entire track carrying our water and some meat. I had forced my change in anger, fought and killed that deviant soul, then raced as fast as I could back to our vehicle, forcing a second change so as to be able to drive; to get back to my mate before he collapsed or worse. I was exhausted and needed a weeks worth of sleep. But he was my first worry. His health has never been strong. Liam had slept like he was comatose all the way home. I had to stay focused and do the driving. Now safely home, I was shaking with exhaustion. I don't think that was a strong enough word for it. But I was also unwilling to enter my bed smelling of that foul wolf we had killed. His scent on my body had kept me agitated enough to make the drive home.

Liam hands me the soft cotton bath towel without saying a word. He knows I heard the conversation between Mark and himself. We may have killed the head of the snake,but the body is still moving around. The body being the drug trade for the zombies. Seriously who thinks of this shit?

Cage fighting with zombies who are on this new drug A-mpd. I'd shake my head, but I am too tired. Apparently they can go twice as fast, have more than just reflex responses and even use weapons once injected with this. Are you freaking kidding me?

Liam takes the towel back from my limp hands and rubs me down with it. Drying my skin while gently tending my sore muscles. Encompassing me in a gentle sweet hug that helps me to loose myself in his scent as I settle my nose in to nuzzle at his neck. My stomach knots loosen as I just breath in the unique masculine odor that is my husband and mate. I need to sleep, to rest. He plants a soft kiss on my shoulder, while steering me to the bed. I practically fall onto our large over sized king bed. He strokes my legs and up my thighs with the towel. Rubbing and gently massaging the muscles still tight and sore. He softly works his way up my back to my shoulders with the towel. Some other time I may be more appreciative of the attention, but right now I am barely conscious. I've hit my proverbial wall. Liam kisses each shoulder before pulling the sheet up and turning the light off.

•••••

Morning comes early. I was hoping to get to sleep in, but not today. An early knock comes on the front door bright and early. Six am. Again. I feel deja vu coming on. Why does Mark seem to enjoy six in the morning? And there better be coffee involved. Liam is up already, dressed in his jeans and T-shirt flipping through the social media feeds, I presume looking for any trace of that boy we found or the wolfs body we left behind. Unlike in so many movies; when we die, we stay in whatever form we were last in. So if we die human that can be a problem. If we die wolf, we are just a dead dog to virtually all of humanity. This can be a good thing however since law enforcement doesn't bother to get involved at that point typically.

Thomas had been killed in his wolf form, so there is no fear of repercussions from law enforcement. But we did have other issues at hand. It would seem that this Thomas, from the conversation I had mostly overheard, not only had subjugated wolves to do his bidding, but his bidding had included drug trafficking of the new A-mpd coming over the border along with the human trafficking we already knew about. Most was rumored to be going down into the San Diego Los Angeles area. But new rumors have surfaced about using these hyper jacked up more lethal than before Myrna zombie's as cage fighters. I mean, I guess it's better than cock fighting, which for some reason is still a thing in this day and age. It's not like a Myrna can be any more dead, can they?

Chapter 24
Finding Comfort

I sip my coffee while sitting in our big overstuffed swivel rocker with my feet pulled up. Six am should be illegal. Liam is making small talk, chit chat with Mark until I have ingested at least a full third of my cup of java. Both men still standing between me and the front door. Most often when two wolves get together who are of similar dominance, there is a bit of bristling and snapping. Over the years Mark and Liam have found their sweet spot. Mark is comfortable in the knowledge that neither Liam nor I want to take over his pack and they have enough human heart to control any overt impulses that might crop up from time to time. As dominant am I am, both know they can't out maneuver me nor want to.

At some subtle cue that my caffeine meter has been fed, both men discontinue their conversation and look over at me.

"What?" I look up at them. "We have a couch and chairs so sit." I say with no push of authority. Smirking they both take seats, Liam to my left on the wide arm of my current seat leaning into me, Mark on the middle of the couch.

"Congratulations on your kill." Mark leads off with. "Both the Phoenix pack and the Sonora packs are grateful to you. We let them know where to find the remains. We believe the boy you mentioned…" His brows furrow darkly "was another runaway or escapee, like our Isaac and Ramon. So they will be collecting his remains as well" The room falls silent for a moment. The slam of a door alerts us one of my boys is up and about.

I yell down the hall "Be dressed, we have a guest."

"Yes mom, I can smell him." Jack responds. I smile into my coffee. My boys have transitioned into werewolves more easily and readily than I believed they would. No outbursts of temper or random partial changes even when a game of Monster Mob 3 gets out of hand. Mark hasn't formally accepted them into the pack, which may eventually be a problem. With four of us now, not officially pack but a family unit there will come a time something may have to change. I'm just not sure what. Mark won't willingly give up his pack nor should he and I don't want to move to a state that has no formal packs. The ones that generally don't have formal packs, also don't tend to have the government zombie contracts either. So no work-ee no pay-ee.

Mark smiles absently for a moment enjoying our brief interchange, then squares his shoulders as if ready to do battle. "Do you want the bad news or the …. badder news".

Heaving a sigh I look to Liam allowing him to take the lead here.

"May as well hear it all, don't you think?" Liam prompts. Mark flicks his gaze to his hands resting in his lap, as if wishing for a cup of coffee simply to occupy them.

"Well, the drugs are going through downtown Phoenix, where apparently they are operating some kind of death match Myrna style. Which we pretty much knew" Marks tension is beginning to rise. "What it seems we didn't know, until this morning, is that they have taken a few wolves along the way, to pit against them in a horrible

Thunder Dome kind of scenario!" Mark's anger gets the better of him and he rises to begin pacing our living room.

"Anthony's disappeared as you know, but Bethy thinks she knows where he is, since downtown is basically her hunting ground. More concerning is Ron and Jean have disappeared after finding the drug trail leading back to this group. I need for you to make several small excursions and confirm that this is where they are, then report back to me..." Mark stops and takes a breath realizing he has just given orders to Liam and me. Liam stiffens a little looking at me. I am less inclined to take offense because quite frankly I intended to hunt this group of individuals down regardless of permission. Having it, just makes it safer for everyone involved. I shrug. An audible sigh from Mark signals we can continue the conversation.

"I was under the impression we had concluded Ron and Jean were not hunting because they were flipping houses and very successfully in this market. Not involved in any nefarious plots." Liam brings up. Mark's expression changes to one of exasperation.

"I thought you two weren't pack?" Throwing his hands up in exasperation "How is it you have the poop scoop almost before I do? I just found out about them a few days ago" He asks. Liam and I exchange a look and quick grin. Having our teenagers being besties with the packs two teenagers means information tends to flow pretty rapidly. I don't think much is secret really between those four. And they say girls have a blabber mouth.

Shaking his head a bit but still smiling he continues "Well they noticed in some of the historic district houses a pretty damning evidence trail of vagrancy and started poking around. Of course they were thinking only to prevent damage to their properties, but what they found was more evidence of this trafficking and A-mpd drug ring." He pauses taking a breath."You were going to go hunting anyway, weren't you?" We smirk in unison. Jack comes around the corner.

"Hey Mark, going hunting? Where and why?"He asks looking at us innocently. Liam sighs heavily while Mark seems to find it amusing that my eighteen year old son is asking about hunting A-mpd up Myrna's, murdering werewolves and missing pack members. I however, am not amused.

"You... Go.... Out... This is not your business." I say trying to put enough authority in my voice he'll listen without having to use a push of the wolf to enforce it. Jack locks eye to eye with me, his wolf gold shifting in the iris then back to his usual hazel green. He heard the order and chose to obey it rather than test me. Blinking and turning his head to break the stare down, Jack turns slightly to look at Mark saying simply "Call me if you need Patrick and I". He turns and walks out of the room.

Putting his head down to mine, Liam softly says "Some day dear, that's not going to work." Though his tone is quiet, it doesn't quite conceal the concern he feels. Jack and I have already butted heads a few times and neither of us is good at backing down apparently. A fight between the two of us, would not end well. Jack's young and strong and seems to have inherited a lot of my overt dominance.

Clearing his throat, Mark breaks through the moment and attempts to redirect our discussion back to planning.

"We need to get downtown. Have eyes on the building. Ensure it's the right one. Bring the pack in and lock this down." Mark pauses. His nerves once again seem to be getting the better of him and I can see his mind racing "This has to stop. Here. No one involved can slip through" Looking at both of us he continues "Being outside of pack there's a lot you can accomplish that I can not. If I go, it's automatically assumed the packs intent is to fight. If I send anyone, it's the same situation, or worse. They could end up disappearing like Anthony".

Liam sits upright with a frown "So if we disappear its okay? I'm not clear on this."Liams voice is clipped and there's a note of anger building behind his comment. His straight back and shoulders are an early warning he is getting agitated. I put my hand on his thigh and give a small sub-vocal hum to calm him. Softly I add "I don't think that's what he meant."

Jack and Patrick come into the room and sit on the floor cross legged, sipping what I presume to be juice from the smell. Both boys are wearing their pajama bottoms and not much else. Hair is still bed head uncombed. Their intent to support their father is not a good thing right now. Mark's focus changes and he brings himself to the balls of his feet. Crap, this is not how we need to be handling this.

I practically whisper "Boys, take yourselves out of here slowly and without looking the alpha in the eye. You just changed the dynamics in the room." Keeping my hand on my husband "This is not the time or place. Mark we are not challenging you. The boys are just being a bit overprotective. It's good, it's all good." Both boys stand slowly keeping their heads turned off to the side. Liam watches them go, a good sign he's no longer focused on Mark. I guess yesterday is still a bit fresher than I thought, or Mark anticipated.

As the boys exit the room, Mark slowly forces himself to sit back down and breaths out a long breath he had been holding. Rolling his shoulders to release the tension, Mark remains seated. Liam blinks several times as if momentarily dazed then excuses himself, following the boys.

"I'm sorry. I don't usually let things escalate like that." Mark's nostrils are still flaring just a tiny bit, so I wait before responding.

Keeping my head down I say into my rapidly cooling coffee "You have nothing to apologize for, but thank you. You are correct in giving us sanction to find these dogs and hunt them. But it will take the strength of the pack to eliminate the threat. Liam is the better tracker but in wolf form I can hold them, make them submit, for the pack to take justice." I look at Mark gauging his emotions. "Let Liam and I make two excursions. First to confirm the place they are keeping these fights at. Make sure it's not multiple locations and the like. Then we can set Bethy to watch for their next event. She can call us when it's occurring. Her scent shouldn't send up any red flags as that's her and Ilya's normal hunting ground. Once she calls, I'll shift to my wolf and we'll come down there. Liam can call and you bring in the cavalry in the form of the pack in both wolf and human guise and of course I'll leave it to you to notify the Crow's Nest as well." Mark's nodding his head as I lay out the plan, in what seems like agreement.

"Yes, and the Crow's Nest will have to take custody of any and all involved including wolves, not just the dead." He says.

I still have friends on the force even though I am technically retired. A few who work for the werewolf division of law enforcement that we call The Crow's Nest are often helpful sharing information. My own brother Joshua is on the job where he lives as well, in Northern California and we too share information, gathered intelligence and data on a regular basis.

Being the Alpha Mark feels a desire to punish the individuals involved in this himself. But he is a kind man at heart and wouldn't be able to follow through I think. At least not without some damage to his soul. Me personally on the other hand, not so much. I'd be happy to do some punishing but it's not my pack. Also, by adding local law enforcement into the mix we ensure their continued trust and cooperation.

We spend a bit more time working out the details and minutia. I can hear my boys still in the kitchen, but know I will have to go find Liam and make peace. Standing up Mark looks towards the depth of the house. "I am sorry I caused a rift. That wasn't my intent." I can tell he wants to say more, but instead he gently grabs the door knob to go. Pausing again, he looks as if he is weighing what to add to his last statement. Through pursed lips he shakes his head instead just taking his leave, closing the door softly behind him.

Taking a deep breath, I slowly get up from the chair and make my way to the kitchen. Both boys are still seated at the dinette bar. They don't say a word munching on slightly under cooked eggs and sausage, simply look from me to our bedroom in the back of the house where their dad is. "We'll discuss this later." I say gently. Passing through to the bedroom, I close the door to give our conversation at least a semblance of privacy. Liam is still mad. I can smell it permeating the room. His anger seems a bit out of proportion to the discussion we had been having. It's not just the anger, it's the fear I can smell underneath that, that seems to be driving him. We both know this is not some fly by night operation.

There is money involved and several wolves who may or may not be a part of Marks pack that Mark had seemed blissfully unaware of. We both know people are going to die. People we know and probably like. But such is life, even outside of a werewolf pack. Bad people die.

Walking further into the bedroom Liam is just sitting on the edge of the bed. Taking a seat next to him I wait. He looks smaller and more defeated than normal to my eye. I've always held that killing our own is demoralizing and psychologically damaging. Being in law enforcement long enough to retire from it, gave me a bit more of a personal insight. It's one thing to stop a bad buy or even kill a Myrna once in a zombie state. Your mind knows it's a good thing, a positive task with only the righteous as an outcome. But going after your own, werewolves who not only drug the dead and pit them against themselves but other werewolves as well, that is a different matter. No less righteous of course but maybe a little more of that gray area. The shading leaves room for doubt. Who all will be involved? Will we have to kill wolves simply because they have been bitten by the Myrna's? What about our boys? There is no way they won't become involved on some level if we are.

After a while we lean into each other rubbing shoulder to shoulder in support and comfort. I relay the final plans Mark wants of both of us as well as the pack. Liam listens in silence. Us touching is soothing to both my mate and myself. Wolves greet each other by rubbing along their muzzles down their necks to their shoulders. And humans, especially babies, get a calming effect from touch as well. Werewolves crave touch and it's one of the reasons we don't do well alone for very long. Mated pairs crave to be in each others presence like peanut butter and jelly. Talking through the plans with my mate calms him, reassures him and steadies him.

"I will always be with you" I say, adding "I promise." The stress of the last couple of days hunting one of our own, knowing we were going to kill him has put an edge on both of us. Knowing this hunt is as likely to result in more werewolf deaths hasn't allowed my mate to settle any further. Mark's seemingly careless comments only served to escalate the danger our entire family could be in. Add to the mix how dominant I am, my mate is feeling he needs to protect not only me but our relatively newly changed children and tempers almost got out of hand. It wouldn't be the first time werewolves have fought and died over something stupid.

"I love you" He replies and nuzzles deeper into my neck bringing with him the scent of arousal. Smiling we embrace. His nuzzle becomes more insistent and my body reacts to his desire. Knowing at our age the comfort of our mates body along with the deeper satisfaction of total acceptance. The eager touches and ardent replies.

Even though it was still morning, early even by some standards we enjoy each others bodies. Soothing the last few days and weeks mental stresses and physical exertions. The little zing of the first mornings caffeine now being put to much more sensual use. Afterwards Liam falls back asleep. His shoulders more relaxed, his wounded shoulder red from healing with his change. The gentle drift and scent and sound lulling me as well. I will never leave him. I love him. Next to my children he is my everything.

Later is a better time for plans, discussions and worries.

Chapter 25
Don't Argue With The Alpha Bitch

A few weeks have gone by and our initial excursion was successful in telling us where our problem wolves are holding these modern day cage fights. Bethy was assigned to keep watch and just today let everyone know apparently the game is on. Maybe they haven't heard their insane leader has been killed. Maybe they don't care. More worrisome is maybe he wasn't in fact the leader. But regardless, the Phoenix Pack has made it their goal to end this barbaric evil blood sport in their territory.

It was decided that the Crow's Nest would not be notified until it was all over and decisions could be made. How many wolves would be found, how many A-mpd Myrna's needed identifying after being put down. And all the other details we are sure will need to be attended to. Ellan and I are called by Mark shortly before noon letting us know today's the day. Our boys, of course, want to help they say. It almost comes down to a dominance match between Jack and Ellan. Finally I intercede by calling Mark back, telling him I am sending the boys to him. That they are to stay human. But that they can help with the cleanup after, and only after any fighting is done.

We get off the freeway at 7th Ave and make our way to the garage we know is being used as the entry point to the fights. It took almost two weeks to slowly identify the exact location, to insure there weren't others and set Bethy to watch in such a way that nothing was disturbed.

The streets, normally littered with the homeless are oddly empty, especially for midday. Many of the downtown streets are one way so to accommodate parking our van, we find an empty slot by a favored restaurant pub we enjoy, O'Collins. The plus is, it's only two blocks from where we are needed to be. It's early yet on this Sunday, so they aren't open and parking is easily accessible on the street. Once the pub opens and night falls this is still a busy restaurant with live music and an overflow of people. Ellan has shifted back at the house to make things easier. Her extra clothes, should we need them, safely tucked into the hidden cargo storage along with water, dried beef and shoes. I am wearing my normal attire along with a favorite knife I have sheathed at my side. Guns are great but they generally don't do enough damage to stop a Myrna and have proven ineffectual against the drugged up versions. This makes our task that much more dangerous. Now, instead of stopping the dead from a distance, it has to be up close and very personal giving the dead a chance to return the favor.

We make our exit onto the street. No one seems to be around. City streets are a bit eerie when deserted. Quickly we catch the scent not just of multiple wolves but that overwhelming scent of death and decay that is the hallmark of Myrnas as well.

"I wonder were everyone parks? I mean I can smell over a dozen wolves, shouldn't there be cars? We aren't that far."I ask. Ellan just looks at me in silence. It doesn't seem high on her priority list at the moment. She pads off eastward towards the crosswalk passing the hotel signage indicating the entrance that is above the pub from an antique elevator or stairway. The whole building was built back over a hundred years ago in the 1930's. It's clearly seen better days. It is not only still standing but being in operation as a tourist attraction is a testament to it's strength and resilience.

Crossing the street we walk past the empty skyscraper. A forty story building of glass and steel that once housed differing banks and business' and has stood empty for the better part of 25 years once the banking giant left the down town. It's still fenced off, showing signs of heavy neglect and disuse.

Ellan follows the scent trail past the decaying hulk to another seeming disreputable structure immediately next to it, a 4 story parking garage. Approaching, the sound of the crowd evident to our wolf ears. Most of the homeless have clearly avoided the area whether out of habit or fear of something bad happening to them in this typical old block building, only lightly graffitied which in itself is odd. Clearly the Urban Renewal Department has missed this entire block, or just failed to care about it. The whole area seems more deserted and empty than you'd imagine the downtown of a major metropolitan area should be.

Ellan and I approach the building with caution looking around seeking a quiet entry point. I am on two feet and Ellan on four, her anger becoming more and more palpable like a cloak I can almost see or feel. Seems stupid and careless or arrogant to not have a lookout for an illegal cage fight but nothing causes either of us to feel as if we are being watched or fear discovery. Maybe they don't know their head honcho, Thomas has been killed. Maybe they just presume him out hunting rather than dead.

I can hear the deep rumble of a growl starting from Ellan. Reaching down, I brush her shoulder with a light touch to reassure and sooth her. The anger is not easily soothed. We travel down a level and find the cars I had wondered about earlier. Here I can discern a few cars I know, but the majority of them I am not familiar with. Yet. I inhale deeply taking into my nasal cavity those scents which aren't familiar, closing my eyes allowing my wolf sense to memorize them in case we need to know later. Re-opening my eyes I see what has hold of my mates interest. Along the north facing wall is a door, metal and brand shiny new in this apparently abandoned structure.

The scent of Myrnas is seeping from the cracks of the closed and sealed shiny new door. It is almost overwhelming to my senses even though the door is closed tightly, almost. I can imagine it's whats triggering Ellan's continued chest deep vibrations I know to be a low snarl. Even in human guise I find I prefer to mouth breathe, the odor becomes so strong. My mate leads the way towards the doors that glisten with cleanliness and a slight tangy sharp odor of new welds, clearly out of place with the rest of the surroundings. Here, a pair of wolves in human guise stand outside; relaxed, bored even, texting on their phone links and not paying attention. Having acute senses means very little if you are too stupid to use them.

"Give me a sec" I whisper softly, going down to one knee and checking my own phone. "Okay the boys and the pack are almost parked, they should be no more than two minutes behind us, do you want to wait for them? To go in, in force?" Ellan pulls in a deep breath and begins to move forward. "Or not" sighing I put my phone away and stand.

Ellan stalks up to these two acting as guards, stiff legged with her head lowered, ears pinned back. Unleashing her force of will, she gives them more than a taste of her dominance and power. Being lesser wolves, and they are all lesser wolves compared to my mate, they both fall to their knees not offering any resistance. While I pat them down, clearing them of weapons and zip tie their hands behind their backs Ellan bites clean thru their electronics rendering them useless.

"Now be good boys and wait here for my sons to come take you into custody. Make any warning attempts and she will kill you without a second thought" The younger of the two can't even bring himself to look at me, maybe he is too new or far enough down in structure to understand his situation but the older male, typical of the harder more high ranking wolves, makes a feeble attempt to growl at me. One quick glare and rumble from Ellan stops the sound before it can escape. He turns his head, offering his throat in placation. The human form often can overrule the wolf dominance structure but Ellan is not playing and this one needs to learn and be dealt with.

I open the door as softly as I can, which with these new doors is actually quite easy. None of the inside participants seem to notice, or if they do, their brains don't register that the new players are not a part of their group. The stench from the Myrnas is somehow even more overwhelming. It would easily cause a sensitive nose to deaden after a short time. It's no wonder these wolves are oblivious to our arrival.

Overhead are typical fluorescent light bars. On portable rollers are additional large LED flood lights clearly illuminating the giant caged ring arena. On the outside of the welded bars are about thirty or so wolves all in human guise making bets, drinking and doing multitudes of illegal substances. The stench isn't just Myrna's but sweat, blood, and urine as well as excitement, anger, fear and pain. Such a miasma is turning my stomach. I can imagine Ellan must be feeling its affects as well.

On a darkened wall to my left is a bank of tiny two foot by two foot by six foot cages each holding an enraged Myrna. And to my right I see a bank of larger cages, not so much cages as reinforced aluminum airline crates filled with those prisoners in their wolf form. At least four that I can discern. My nose isn't good enough to determine if Ron or his mate Jean are among those in the cages. We walk unimpeded towards the center of the room. Ellan leads by a few steps into the ring where the light is brightest. Two sides are open at the moment as it appears we came during a break in the action. Money is passing hands as freely as is the booze and drugs. The floor of the ring is slick with body fluids. Being dragged by a pair of wolves in human guise with snare poles around the neck is a Myrna doing its best to reach either of its captors. A third one grabs one of the flailing arms and injects a whitish drug hurriedly from a pressure syringe. I presume this is the new A-mpd we've been told about. With morbid fascination I watch as the Myrna goes completely limp within a few seconds. At the same time a pair of wolves in human guise are pulling out a wolf from one of the metal cages using the threat of multiple bang sticks to control it.

Ellan's rage and fury unleashes itself as she stands center stage under the stark piercing lights. Though she's made no obvious outward show of aggression, her force of will, power and dominance radiate so clearly that every wolf's attention is immediately drawn to her even over the other noise's made by the maddened Myrnas or stench in the building. Regardless of form, every wolf drops to their knees, and the lesser wolves, even further to the ground. Some even give their bellies to the alpha bitch now clearly in control of this room of deviant rogues. I step away from my mate with difficulty and begin restraining the in human guise wolves. Only being Ellan's mate and my human logic keeps me on my feet and moving with purpose. I am not immune to her power, I just realize her rage and command of subservience is not directed at me, and so my wolf's instincts allow me to start my task of restraining the others.

I only recognize a couple of the wolves as pack, so I am relieved not too many seem to have fallen into such deviant behavior. In a few moments several more wolves can be heard approaching the entry from our local pack. Mark has brought those he can trust as well as our boys. All who have come to the warehouse to help clear the room and deal with the vileness contained within. However Ellans clear rage and power are making that task very difficult for them. Mark, still standing outside the room clears his throat so as to not startle anyone. Ellan whips around letting a deep snarl rip from her throat while exposing her eye teeth even further. Mark drops to one knee head bent but still on his feet. Jack is standing beside him.

"We need you to take it down a bit. Maybe even step out so we can detain these assholes and find out who the victims are here." He says, looking only at his knee. I stand frozen. Tense. Ready to step in if she decides she is not ready to acquiesce her control. But it would seem she has decided to let Mark and the pack handle it. Giving a large sneeze and head shake Ellan gradually stalks past us with still raised neck fur and hackles, out the double doors. Its as if the room itself breaths a sigh of relief.

I follow her out handing off my remaining zip tie cuffs to Mark nodding to him. "Make sure you finish that Myrna on the catch poles, she's been injected with the A-mpd and is about to become very dangerous" Mark acknowledges it and immediately enters the room to finish the many tasks at hand. Outside the garage, in the full light of day breathing becomes easier without the cloying miasma of Myrna smell or any of the fear and adrenaline musk of other wolves. Ellan has stepped out to the roadway to let the pack take over control and allow her push of power to subside. She very rarely uses her force of will and dominance in such a large and overt display. But today it was needed. She is sitting on the black tarred asphalt which has to be hot. "Hey baby doll, lets go back to the vehicle and cool down and get some fuel." I say, running my hand down her head and shoulders affectionately. In clear agreement she gets up and pads westward the two blocks back, to where we have parked the van earlier to begin this hunt.

"There's that awesome Irish pub we like right there, underneath the old hotel. We parked right by it. Want to change and get some late lunch? You have to be starving by now." She looks up at me and I can tell the use of her power has taken a bit more of a toll on her than either of us cares to admit, she is tired. Probably wouldn't be able to shift quite as quickly as I am used to seeing. Might not be able to shift at all until fueled back up. Patrick passes us while working with the pack members to help round up this mess. Since both are so newly turned we told them to stay human for more control and better ability to help.

"Is mom okay?" Patrick asks. He can see her step is a bit slower and less purposeful.

"Yeah, she'll be fine. It went pretty much as we thought. But you still need to be careful. These idiots are capable of anything if they are willing to pit their own against drugged up freaking zombies. Jack's already inside" Ellan winds her way across her son's thigh in a sign of affection more suited to a cat, but letting him know she's okay.

We continue heading back towards the van. It was a good day. I guess. We stopped an insane cage fighting Myrna vs werewolf for profit drug ring. But we seriously needed to have a talk with Mark when this was all over. How was it even conceivable this went unnoticed, downtown?

The cute little pub, now opening up, offers a small row of outside seating and we choose the two-seater closest to the end. My back is to the colorful stained glass window that has beautiful four leaf clovers and pints of deep dark ale's along with a harp. The door is old and heavy and worn from many decades of use. We know from previous visits the food to be good and the beer better. The server doesn't even bat an eye at Ellan sitting almost daintily (don't tell her I said that) on the one wooden bench. I order two plates of corned beef cabbage and two chicken pot pies. This is Bethy's teams territory for hunts so the wait staff must be used to seeing werewolves around, even if she is a bit on the smaller side for a wolf.

While waiting for our meal Ellan's ears perk up and her nose points towards the chaos we just left. A growl starts deep in her throat startling some of the other patrons. I look that direction but can't see or hear anything in this form. In my head I hear *guard the hotel, its in danger.* Ellan leaps over me and the railing, landing at a run towards the fight we thought was over.

Chapter 26
Zombies Don't Make Good Hotel Guests

I get up, turning to enter the hotel when I see the cargo elevator's brass doors have opened and a trail of A-mpd up zombies have bolted up the narrow carpeted steps next to it, towards the guest rooms. This hotel is a popular tourist site, claiming to be haunted and still decorated in its mostly original and now shabby 1940s and 50s motif.

I follow the pack of stinking things up the stairs taking out my Arkansas toothpick, a lovely remarkably sharp blade. Ellan often says its more suited to a renaissance festival with its brass head and guard, glossy wooden handle and leather sheath. But its nine inch blade will be more than adequate for what I need to accomplish right now. One at a time I get behind the last in the line and am able to thankfully slice all the way through their neck due to their advanced decaying flesh, though the stench is overwhelming to my nose. My blade is sharp, I am strong and fast and they are otherwise occupied chasing some imaginary foe only they can hear. I've managed to drop three by the time we reach the first landing which is actually the second floor.

A lone straggler veers off for some reason and goes tripping down the loose carpet of the hallway falling to the ground. Unable to re-balance itself enough to get up, it falls as easy prey to my blade. My inner wolf is very happy with this work and I feel a push of adrenaline that energizes me to continue pursing the remaining zombies.

Screams from above tell me that the hotel patrons are not as smart as I could have hoped for and have not sought refuge in their rooms. I pull on my wolf further. Sprinting up the second floor steps to the third. There I find several have broken from the now smaller pack to focus their deadly intent on the remains of what momentarily ago, was clearly a lovely young sun bather most likely headed to or from the fourth floor rooftop pool. These three zombies are engaged in what their movie predecessors typically depicted; the feeding pattern. On their knees grasping at the entrails now streaming in brightly red ribboned trails. The messy event so new the body still smells alive to me.

Guessing from the young ladies facial expression of surprise rather than fear or pain, I'm not even sure she realizes she is dead yet. My blade quickly dispatches the two zombies with their backs to me, their heads virtually coming unattached only being held on by some skin and ligament remnants. The third Myrna zombie stops gorging itself long enough to open its foul mouth and scream like the mummy/zombie creature from that Brandon Fraser move of the late 90's. I have just a moment to think how weird, I would never have guessed that to be what was real from that movie. Swinging my blade in a downward arch that is lent speed and strength from my wolf, and it is forever silenced.

Turning around, I slip in the gore momentarily and let loose a snarl from my still human throat. The stairs leading to the final fourth floor landing are oddly quiet and I take them two at a time. Reaching the landing I can see the door to the pool standing open and the remaining drug fueled Myrna's are literally bouncing off the walls. Like a bad game of ping pong, only avoiding the pool because of the secondary safety gate. If I can open that gate and trap them up there, I can pick them off later or at least more safely.

A few guests, for some unknown reason, come out of their rooms drawing attention to us. *Always helps when people volunteer to become zombie snack***s** I think sarcastically. I push past the four fast zombies who are still in their drug fueled state. A quick flip to raise the latch, shove open the pool gate and give a loud yell. Well, that was the plan. Sounded good in my head. I got as far as the gate and realized it needed a key card to release the latch and my yell was more of a cough as my body finally caught up to my brain and asked what the hell did I think I was doing. The four zombies filled the small entry space between the hotels exterior door and the access gate causing the latch to simply give way due to our combined overwhelming weight. I stumble out onto the cool deck area of the patio tripping, dodging and pushing these melting gooey bodies from getting too close to me to bite or rend my flesh.

Crap I think. *I'm in trouble now.* I hop onto a nearby table but it can't hold my weight and I come crashing down under its antique metal umbrella, which has afforded me some shielding from the four remaining Myrna's now intent upon my destruction. One Myrna manages to impale itself on the bent leg of the table and I reach over and slice its neck cleanly. Okay, good one down. But I am scrambling backwards quickly as the other three seem to have found a renewed zeal and form a circle around me, or maybe its just because the circular metal umbrella style top is giving them direction. Their grasping hands and snapping jaws would do a horror movie justice and I am stuck in the middle. I've had to drop my knife in favor of holding onto my new found shield. My inner wolf is wanting to snap back at them but somehow I don't think this is a good game plan.

The slick surface of the metal is hot and their flesh peels away from their bodies as they push and rub against the roughened edges trying to make me their next meal. One in particular is shrieking and clacking its teeth on the metal, its body bent practically in half. If I didn't need both hands to hold this thing, I could reach around and finish it off. I squirm over slowly towards the pool hoping to drop them in there, giving me a chance to regroup and finish them which works partly.

Two fall into the water flailing and splashing, not aware of whats happened. The third is a bulldog not being distracted or led. I'm no longer strong enough to push both the fighting Myrna and the metal table top into the pool so I have to make do as best I can. Apparently this pool is old enough to have a diving depth and the two who did fall in, thrash their way into the deep end and sink below the surface.

I'm tired. I hadn't eaten or refueled before this round two of drugged super-Myrna zombie round up began and while it's only been a few minutes I'm sure, the adrenaline as well as the physical climb of stairs, running and slicing through flesh is not as easy as it looks. I am growing tired and my reflexes are slowing, my chest hurts, my ears are ringing and this reflective heat on the rooftop is sapping what little dexterity I have left. I am starting to pant as well telling me I better do something quick or this fight will end badly for me. Somewhat tossing, somewhat dropping the hot metal umbrella top, I make an attempt to reach the far side of the pool, close to the edge of the building. Maybe I can push it into the pool or over the edge.

Surprisingly, the railing at this side of the rooftop pool deck is only four feet high with a pretty turquoise planter a mere eighteen additional inches of barrier from literally falling off this roof. Briefly I wonder how building codes haven't flagged that one. In too short a time period the Myrna, who is quicker than I wanted to believe, is grappling with me and it's all I can do to keep myself from going over the edge with a forty foot drop or into the literal deep end of the pool where her two compatriots though submerged, are very much still active and willing to tear me apart. My leg gives out and I control the fall to my knee keeping myself both upright and in control of the fetid creatures hands at least. And then I see her.

Out of the corner of my eye, I know it's her. Who else could it be? Ellan leaps the short security fence rather than going around it making a straight path to us. I can see a lot of blood on her brown coat, with a skin flap exposed on her hip that has to pain her. There is a piece of her ear missing as well, with blood squirting enough to leave a trail as if to help her find her way back.

But she only has eyes for the Myrna I am in a life and death grapple with. She leaps again, over a corner of the pool keeping to her straight line and grabs the distracted Myrna by the throat. Planting both front and back feet on the planters rim, bunching her muscles she launches herself over the edge dragging the easily one hundred seventy pounds of struggling flailing body with her. I can hear her growl and feel her anger and outrage as she sails past. All time has stopped as I watch her with her prey stop their outward movement over the railing into the air like some sick Saturday morning cartoon and they fall. I can't even scream.

I race to the railing, my jaws snapping despite being in human guise, my hands grasping at the air as if I could stop it from happening even though it's already happened. Watching her and her prey plummet to the earth hitting the ground four stories below. I don't know how long I stared at their broken and lifeless forms. Even in death, she still held a grip on the now immobile Myrna.

A crowd is beginning to gather after the initial shock of seeing the two locked together fall to earth. Cell phones out and busy as always. Most trained on the bloody scene but a few have swept up to catch me still immobilized by shock, staring down at the remains of my mate. Slowly I tip my head up to the sky and a low long mournful sound of abject misery rips from my throat.

Chapter 27
Love Lost

Coming from a human throat the sound doesn't quite have the quality of a howl, but it conveys the meaning clearly. Being on the rooftop of the building allows my voice to travel further than it might normally and soon a few others within ear shot, not involved in a life and death fray, join in. Though human ears might not hear, them I do.

Bethy has found her way onto the rooftop and either witnessed or understood what has occurred. Hopping onto the decorative planter, she takes my hand between her front teeth exerting only minimal pressure trying to guide, not order. Her body language is clear with tucked tail, dropped ears and lowered stance. Placing her body between mine and the railing, she whines softly while gently using her shoulder to ensure I don't follow my mate. My mind is completely and utterly blank. A moment later I step back from the railing and walk slowly to the door returning into the hotels less well lit hallway. What few guests there are give me wide berth, knowing in the primordial portion of their brains, that I am not to be bothered. Bethy is beside me, her shoulder rubbing my knee, concern in her every line. I follow the hallway to the stairs, the loose carpet no longer a concern of mine.

The dead Myrna's are beginning to look like grotesque figures in an old fashioned who-dun-it from the 1940s décore. Their black gore soaking unrepentant into the old worn carpeting. The open stairwell seems darker, quieter somehow mourning with me. At the time I didn't realize there was a beautiful carved wooden railing with brass fittings. Now I use it, holding on to it, like the old man I am. I can hear my breath wheezing in my ears. I reach the bottom landing entering the hotel's check in and entry area; moving slowly somehow swimming through the motions. More dead Myrnas litter here along with a dead wolf. I don't think I know him. I move onto the street, making my way to Ellan's body and the gawkers that always seem to follow tragedies. Bethy is again gently pushing at my side trying to move me on, from letting the grief overwhelm me. The dead Myrna's goo is oozing all over my beautiful mates muzzle and head. Her teeth still firmly closed on the almost disconnected portion of the neck. On her way down she still managed to shake this creature to ensure it didn't survive.

The fall itself would not have likely stopped the drug crazed zombie so she knew to protect everyone she had to kill it midair, mid fall. She had to know she herself couldn't have survived that fall. We wolves really are not indestructible. Not at all like the novels and movies make us out to be. Bethy's wolf places herself between me and the bodies when I would have bent down to clean off her beautiful muzzle. She softly whines, a sound of sympathy and concern. I hear someone come up behind me and the wolf around my legs tense's up. Partially turning, still unable to pull myself from my dead mate, I see Joseph approach us. His face is dirt streaked. Gore covers his clothes and he has a look of loss also on his face. Joseph is a mid level wolf much like myself, even though he is considered third and normally in different circumstances we would bristle a bit for control of the conversation.

Today, we are both too tired and worn to care. Our wolf natures accepting neither is in a position to threaten or be threatened. Stopping a respectful distance Joseph says "Mark's dead, his second Jim is as well. I'm not sure what happened but it appears there was another whole room of cages of those damn A-mpd zombies. We had to kill one of the pack who became infected, and the two guards you had restrained for the same reasons. Your boys are fine, and I am sorry for your loss but we need you to come and make sure there's no additional stupid tax to be paid today among our own. The media appears to have already arrived and the Crows Nest somehow already has people on the ground as well."

"I am not your alpha, nor do I want to be" I say.

"We know Liam, but your boys seem to be taking over things and managing this FUBAR. They aren't pack, even if Mark was helping train them. Someone is bound to become irritated at that.... eventually" He looks me obliquely in the eye but not as a challenge more as a request to make sure none of us loose any more family members today.

I don't know how I am going to make it through this, but I start my body moving towards the scene of slowly organizing chaos to address the issues at hand and to find some solace in the sight of my two children still alive and stepping into what seems to be their new place in the world.

Chapter 28
Life Moves On

No one wanted this meeting but everyone knew it had to happen. The alpha had to be determined before wolves started killing one another randomly. That's what dominants did. Fight for dominance. For control and for the safety of those under them. It had only been two days since the raid on the downtown fighting ring. Forty eight hours was hardly enough time for this, but waiting too long would lead to more death and discord as some wolves struggled to attain a higher standing, and opportunistic wolves might begin to prey on the zeta's. Then there was the potential that outside influences would come in and attempt a coup.

The dead Myrnas had all been scooped up by The Crows Nest, cataloged and cremated as current law dictated. Kill credit had been assigned to the pack as a whole, so there would soon be a free flowing of funds into the packs account. Mark had apparently done an admirable job in regards to setting the packs finances up. Who knew he understood corporate law?

The Phoenix pack was protected and would flourish once again, once a strong leader was chosen and accepted. Business could regain it's usual ebb and flow.

The room fairly bristled with dominant wolves all looking to see who would claim the alpha status, and who might die trying. Staying in human form meant there was more opportunity for verbal discourse rather than bloodshed and since the meeting had been called at our home, and none of us, not my dead mate nor my two sons or myself were technically pack, made it as neutral a place to meet for privacy as pretty much anywhere else. My younger son Jack seems to have taken a spot at the head of the room with his older brother Patrick standing to his right. Psychologically this served as his second. The two so called rescued brothers are sitting together to the left of Jack. I know I know their names, but some things my mind is not really grasping right now. These four are presenting a united front, almost their own pack within a pack.

My wolf is more ascendant than I care to admit and I don't entirely trust myself. The only place I feel calm enough not to revert to my wolf form is here at home where my mates scent is still strong, comforting and easily felt. Every time I leave the house I get panic attacks. My wolf wants to rend and bite until I can once again feel the presence of my mate.

My sons called for the meeting here, with Joe agreeing to it since he was the de facto alpha until such a time as a new leader can be chosen. Joe has previously acknowledged he doesn't want to lead and will support a worthy alpha. He had an immense amount of respect for Mark and grieves him perhaps more so than many in the pack.

Sitting here in our front room, there is a shadow I can almost make out behind Patrick standing off to the side, between us but I'm not really paying attention enough to focus on it. My brain thinks it must be a trick of the noon days full light. Seven lesser wolves, including Bethy sit in the back of the room on the floor, almost as if they hope not to be noticed. Since bloodshed is almost always involved in these kinds of dealings, no non wolves are permitted. Families have to wait at home to know if something affecting their lives has happened. Somehow that doesn't seem fair, but it's safer for all involved this way.

Eleven additional wolves are standing milling about, the remains of Marks original pack. We lost several wolves in the fight to clear our territory of this diseased group of individuals. Both from those involved in the evil and those who were killed or had to be put down. Ellan, upon returning to the abandoned building when further control and containment became necessary, took it upon herself to kill every wolf she ran across who was a part of the participating wolves. This included the wolf who had shot and killed Mark. The clean up team didn't have a full body of that man. And still, our front room seems too small for so many egos and wills.

To help things stay as calm as they ever can, the side tables have been laid out with large slabs of ham, chicken and turkey and an assortment of crackers and cheese. Wolves need fuel.

Jack, clearing his throat, calls the meeting to order and begins by introducing Ramon and Isaac officially. These two wolves, turned against their will, whose parents were killed yet were the catalyst that eventually led us to the revelation of the trafficking and kidnapping-into-cage fighting network. This is something the alpha would typically do but as Mark had already included them in a pack's hunt last month no one seems to get their feelings too hurt over this. There's some head nodding and subdued hello's but no one is too sure where they fall into all of this. Mark had been training them to know the good manners of being a wolf, and he and his wife Cindy had taken them in, but they were never formally made pack. Until now.

"Welcome to our home everyone. Obviously the elephant in the room is who gets to take the seat as alpha with Mark now gone." And quick as that, Danny lunges from the left, stepping in front of both Isaac and Ramon, disregarding them as any threat, making a grab for Jack. His eyes are lit with blood lust and his teeth, human teeth, are exposed in a snarl. Jack turns to meet his attacker, adopting a typical wrestlers' stance when a shot rings out coming from over his left shoulder, momentarily deafening the whole group. Danny falls bleeding out, to the floor. The tiny tear through his cheek and ragged hole forcefully expelled from the back of his skull has caused the big man to collapse to the ground. The pack mate behind him stares blankly in shock. Jack straitens back up and asks if Greg and Kathy, a mated pair of nominally lesser wolves, if they'd mind cleaning up the mess. A random piece of drywall falls almost comically to the floor.

All other movement has ceased temporarily. I stand up, my wife's pistol still in my grip, "If any other wolf here chooses to attack dishonorably, I'll be happy to shoot you too." I may be heartsick over the loss of my mate, but I'll be damned if I allow some witless jackanape to attack my boy with impunity.

Jack turns, looking me over then gives an almost imperceptible nod. Turning back to the room of wolves. "Okay, continuing on."

"What gives you the right to run this meeting? Or even talk about alpha of the pack? Last time I checked you and your family felt they were too good to be pack" David spews, issuing a verbal challenge. A few others nod quietly in agreement. David is an older wolf by most standards, being over forty and having been changed early in life. He's a general laborer which gives his body a lean and taught physique. Having Jack run the meeting and directing the flow is clearly not sitting well with him and has ruffled his feelings.

I take note of who else seems to be agreeing with David's rumblings as I watch the room more closely now for threats. Inhaling deeply, scenting for discord or anger but my nose is less than helpful with the fresh blood still happily congealing on my wife's rug.

Jack continues "I suppose that's a good question. You all know Mark turned both Patrick and I as well as trained us for the time he had. In addition, I don't think there is a wolf here who can dispute my mothers dominance and force of will or that she should have been the rightful alpha had she chosen to take that position."

"Well she didn't and she wasn't and neither are you" David practically spits out, his eyes beginning to shift from his obviously uncontrolled anger. The smell of his hostility agitates a few of the others. The shadow, still just a blur, begins to move towards the angry wolf through the others, who seem oblivious to its presence.

Jack is surprisingly calm and just nods his head in agreement. Patrick, clearly getting agitated as well, glares at David as he rocks from side to side on the balls of his feet. David has distanced himself a bit from the other wolves. Not an easy task to do in this crowded room. The others seem to have given way even though I would consider most of them only mildly dominant wolves. This implies the giving of support or their unwillingness to take sides by giving him space rather than holding him back.

The musk of threat and anger and determination grow with each passing moment.

Patrick starts to step forward, but is held in place by quick a look from Jack.

"If that is a challenge speak the words. Only formal challenge will be accepted." David is practically shaking with the wolfs need to kill once a hunt is begun.

Lifting his lips in a lupine like curled snarl "I David Ember Garcia challenge you Jack hijo de puta Callen for the rights of Alpha to The Phoenix Pack." At the close of the official challenge all of the remaining wolves get as far out of the way as possible, moving furniture with them to create a small clear space in the middle of the room. Ramon and Isaac, not entirely understanding the significance, still step back, their wolves feeling the weight of the challenge.

Patrick lets out a low growl. Still standing I put my hand on his shoulder and whisper "Challenge has been issued. It's a fight between them only."

Jack stands relaxed. David has crouched to grab, with his hands out to his sides. "Don't shoot me old man." he hisses keeping his eyes locked on Jack. There's a gathering of tensions in the room at the implied insult. Several of the lesser wolves flick their gaze to me then back to the two combatants. Everyone's breathing has picked up in anticipation of a bloody brawl. David is considered one of their better fighters. He's lean, mean and fast. Many of the more dominant wolves roll to the balls of their feet in anticipation, feeding off the fear from the lesser ranking ones.

Bethy, Vasili, and Kathy have all inched their way to stand behind me, I presume in support of our claim or perhaps gauging a better set of protectors. It would seem, that the room is split between our eight wolves and the remainder of Marks pack, numbering thirteen. Joseph has bowed his head standing alone off to one side taking neither ours nor David's position.

Having been in law enforcement for years, I can read a room better than most and it's evident that the musky fear, excitement and anxiety are high. If this fight goes on too long, it won't matter who wins, it will become a bar room brawl. Us verses them, only them really aren't the enemy here.

David breaks the stand off by making the first lunge at Jack, snarling and grabbing. Jack takes a single step forward, shifting his balance while drawing in a single deep breath. The order comes with a force of power that rushes through the entire house like a tangible gust of wind "Down..... down now." He says softly.

Practically tripping over himself to stop his forward motion David drops to his knees. His shoulder drops, his hands fall flat on the floor and he tilts his head to the side offering his throat.

Still growling low in his chest Jack cut's even that off. With another dominance laden command of *"stop that."* all sound ceases. The whole room has stopped breathing collectively. The lesser wolves, feeling the push of his commands have taken to their knees as well. Poor Bethy lowest of the ranking pack is in an almost kowtow position. Patrick and I, though behind him, are not completely immune to his command, and have lowered our heads and offered our shoulders in supplication. I didn't realize how strong my son is. When did he know? How did he know? The shadow twines itself around Jack, who appears oblivious to it. While I am immensely proud of him being so like his mother, it causes me concern. Dominant wolves don't always live a long life and are often challenged by others. But he is his mothers son and this is now his pack. Jack casts his eyes around the room making sure no other wolf dares meet his in challenge. Every wolf here keeps their eyes lowered. A small smile has crept onto Josephs face even though he is looking at my tile as if inspecting the grout for cracks. David closes his eyes and relaxes his body. His wolfs acceptance of the alpha's command.

Satisfied that his position is accepted and will no longer be challenged, Jack reigns in his power and control of his wolf. The tensions in the room rapidly shift to its normal levels of musk and scent. The challenge having been duly issued and lost. Accepting of the dominance of Jack, the pack settles in to listen to their new Alpha.

"Now then, if there are no further challenges let's discuss the FUBAR that was two days ago"

Chapter 29

Coming Soon !

The Phoenix pack, led by a young Jack, once again must face new
challenges and new disasters!
Liam must learn how to live without his beloved mate and wife.
And life is about to get very interesting for everyone.

PROMISE OF THE WOLF

Coming in late 2024 to most online retailers

Also by Alice E Wright

The Siberian Cat

The history and detail of how the Siberian cat has traveled and expanded its conquest into our hearts and our homes all over the world. Written with the authors unique and personal knowledge and dedication to the breed for over thirty years. Breeder endorsed, Vet endorsed, reader endorsed – the only book of its kind!

The Raw Facts Of Feline Feeding

The global cat food market in 2021 reached a value exceeding $33 BILLION USD, and promises only to grow. Find out why feeding an obligate carnivore like the animal she is, is more important than ever in today's world. You want the best for your feline companion. This book gives you the knowledge to make the best, most well informed choice for your family. Why are pet foods made the way they are?

Who makes them, who is responsible for them, and how you can do better? Offering raw food to your feline is what she is hardwired for, what her body craves and what makes her thrive. Breeder endorsed, Vet endorsed, owner endorsed!

Pick up your copies today online from most retailers! Ebook and Paperback.